WRITTEN BY **ANDREA BEATY**

**ATT
OF THE FLU
BU**

ACK
UFFY
NNIES

ILLUSTRATED BY **DAN SANTAT**

AMULET BOOKS
NEW YORK

The Library of Congress has catalogued the hardcover edition of this book as follows:

Beaty, Andrea.
Attack of the fluffy bunnies / by Andrea Beaty.
p. cm.
Summary: At Camp Whatsitooya, twins Joules and Kevin and new friend Nelson face off against large, rabbit-like creatures from the Mallow Galaxy who thrive on sugar, but are not above hypnotizing and eating human campers.
ISBN: 978-0-8109-8416-5
[1. Extraterrestrial beings—Fiction. 2. Camps—Fiction. 3. Twins—Fiction. 4. Brothers and sisters—Fiction. 5. Humorous stories—Fiction.] I. Title
PZ7.B380547 Att 2010
[Fic]—dc22

Paperback ISBN: 978-1-4197-0519-9

Text copyright © 2010 Andrea Beaty
Illustrations copyright © 2010 Dan Santat
Book design by Chad W. Beckerman

Printed and bound in U.S.A.
10 9 8 7 6 5 4 3

ABRAMS
THE ART OF BOOKS SINCE 1949

115 West 18th Street
New York, NY 10011
www.abramsbooks.com

For Falana

ACKNOWLEDGMENTS

This one I blame on the Beatys. The millions of hours we spent watching sci-fi movies and British TV shows while consuming mass quantities of buttery popcorn and Pepsi left an enormous mark on my brain (and my waistline). I love you all more than you can know.

Thanks to Michael, Katie, and Andrew for your endless support and supply of chocolate.

Godzilla-size thanks to Susan Van Metre for being the best editor in the universe.

Thanks to my uber-talented agent, Barry Goldblatt, and to Howard, Chad, Jason, Mary Ann, Andrea, Brett, and everyone at ABRAMS. I want you all on my team when the aliens and/or zombies and/or killer chipmunks attack!

And finally, King Kong-size thanks to Dan Santat, who is simply brilliant. Thank you! Thank you! Thank you!

Chapter 1

Meanwhile, in space . . .

The flaming meteor hurtled through the endless, black void. Remember this. It's important later.

Chapter 2

Meanwhile, to begin our story . . .

Not long ago, in a galaxy just beyond the Milky Way—but not quite as far as the Peanut Cluster—there lived a race of fierce, large, ugly, and ferocious furballs known as the Fierce, Large, Ugly, and Ferocious Furballs. (Fluffs for short—though in reality, there is nothing short about Fluffs.)

In fact, Fluffs were (and are) tall with two enormous rabbitlike ears, two enormous rabbitlike feet, two enormous rabbitlike eyes, and one small rabbitlike nose. (Well, they couldn't have two noses. That would be weird.)

Okay, so the Fluffs are rabbits. But they are not mild-mannered, cute-cuddly-carrot-crunching, happy-hopping rabbits like those found on Earth. The Fluffs are fierce warrior rabbits whose long, floppy ears are for slapping. Whose long, floppy feet are for stomping. And whose large eyes spin in opposite directions to hypnotize unsuspecting prey. Oh yeah, and they have fangs.

Fluffs and domestic Earth rabbits is found on the next page in **Table 1: Know Your Fluff,** taken from *The Illustrated Guide to Fluffs and Other Space Creatures You Don't Want to Meet* by Professor Donald J. Dewdy. (Work unpublished.) Go ahead and take a moment to read it, if you want. The rest of us will meet you at the next chapter.

For nonscientifically minded readers, readers who wish they were playing video games right now (you know who you are), and readers forced to read this book for school book reports (so sorry), we'll sum up the contents of Table 1: FLUFFS = BAD.

Go to next chapter.

TABLE 1: KNOW YOUR FLUFF

	EARTH BUNNIES	FLUFFS
Genus	*Sylvilagus floridanus*	*Lepus fluffaricus*
Habitat	Woodlands, meadows, Saturday morning cartoons, pet shops	Fluffs inhabit hot-chocolate marshes on a series of extremely small planets in the Mallow Galaxy. The small, marshmallow-shaped planets have a sucrose-based core and are recognized by their spongy, white—and yummy—surfaces. At the center of the Mallow Galaxy is the Starburst, a large, orange cube-shaped star of sweet candy goodness. The Starburst's radiant energy fuels all life-forms within the Mallow Galaxy.
Diet	Grass, herbs, bunny chow, carrots	Diet? Are you kidding? Who could diet on a marshmallow planet? Fluffs absorb sugary energy through their fine, tubelike clear fur. Fluff fur appears silver-white, but is tinged with pink upon closer inspection. **(WARNING: Closer inspection of a Fluff can be hazardous to your health. Side effects may include but are not limited to: being eaten; being slapped by long, floppy, but surprisingly strong ears; being eaten; being stomped by long, floppy, but surprisingly strong feet; and being hypnotized by large and surprisingly swirly eyes, followed by being eaten.)**

	EARTH BUNNIES	FLUFFS
		Starburst energy supplies all required nutrients to the Fluffs, but they do enjoy the occasional snack when one presents itself (and is too slow, stupid, or spellbound by the Fluffs' swirly eyes to escape). Fluffs are, at present, the only known life-forms left in the Mallow Galaxy. Go figure.
Communication	Nose twitching, tail twitching, extreme cuteness	Mind waves. The hollow tubules of Fluff fur act as telepathic transmitters and receivers. Once transmitted, Fluff brain waves can travel long distances via sweet waves of sugary goodness emitted by the Starburst at the center of the Mallow Galaxy.
Predators	Coyotes, hawks, bob-cats, the Tasmanian Devil, and Elmer Fudd.	Predators? Are you asking what *eats* Fluffs? Ha ha ha ha ha ha ha ha ha ha ha ha ha ha ha ha ha ha . . . snort. . . . That's a good one.

Chapter 3

Remember the flaming meteor hurtling through space from Chapter 1? Here's an update.

Chapter 4

And then . . .

BOOM!

SNIFF *SNIFF*

Chapter 5

"**What's that smell?**" thought Moopsy.*

"It wasn't me," thought Floopsy.*

"Smeller's the feller," thought Cottonswab.*

"Hey!!!" thought Moopsy.

The Fluffs looked at one another. They looked at the planet. They looked at one another again.

"Planet's on fire," thought Floopsy.

"So get a small creature and beat out the flames," thought Cottonswab.

"You ate the last small creature two years ago," thought Floopsy.

"Oh yeah," thought Cottonswab. "That reminds me . . . BUURP."

FWOOSH!

"Did you know burps were flammable?" thought Moopsy.

"EVACUATE!" thought Floopsy.

"EVACUATE!" thought Moopsy.

"BURP!" thought Cottonswab.

*Those of you who skipped Table 1 a few pages back might be wondering why these Fluffs seem to be thinking all the time instead of talking to each other. Hint: It's not because they are smart. This might be a good time for you to go back and read that table before it's too late. We'll take a nap while you read it. Wake us up when you get back.

Chapter 6

Meanwhile, on Earth . . .

The Rockman family van screeched to a halt in front of the crumbling stone arch at the entrance to Camp Whatsitooya. Through the arch, a gravel road wound its way into the dark woods, dwindled to two dirt tracks, and disappeared beyond a half-dead oak tree.

"Out, you two!" said Mr. Rockman. "Time for adventure!"

"Are you sure this is the place?" asked Kevin. "You can't even read that sign, it's old and cruddy and covered with moss or something."

"Of course it's the place," said Mrs. Rockman. "It says so right here on the map."

"And besides, it's not cruddy," said Mr. Rockman. "It's rustic. It says that right here in the brochure. We would never send you to a camp that called itself cruddy."

Mr. Rockman jumped out of the van, sprinted to the back hatch, tossed a mound of camping gear onto the road, sprinted back to the driver's seat, and buckled up again. All in 3.7 seconds flat.

"Yep! Yep! Yep!" said Mrs. Rockman, snapping her fingers excitedly. "We're here, darlings! Oh, summer camp! Beautiful summer camp! Swimming! Hiking! Campfires and marshmallows! I could linger here all day just breathing in the forest air. . . . Well, time's ticking. Off you go!"

Joules and Kevin Rockman climbed out of the van and stood in the ankle-high weeds at the edge of the road.

"Don't you want to come with us to check in?" asked Joules. "You know, just to make sure it's okay."

"Of course it's okay," said Mr. Rockman. "It says so in the brochure. See? 'Camp Whatsitooya, nestled on the aromatic shores of Lake Whatsosmelly. Camp Whatsitooya: Exceptionally Exceptional Outdoors Experiences Guaranteed. No Exceptions.*'"

Joules and Kevin groaned. What kind of person would write that stuff?

"And they have a spa," said Mrs. Rockman. "See? There's even a picture!"

---

*Possible exceptions include, but are not limited to, poison oak, poison ivy, ivy league, little league, 20,000 leagues under the sea, sea sickness, seesaws, spider bite, snake bite, trilobite, and overbite. Results may vary. Guarantee not valid in Illinois, Kentucky, Pennsylvania, or any other state.

"It's an outhouse," said Joules.

"It's rustic!" said her mother. "What could be better?"

Joules and Kevin could each think of at least four hundred and seven thousand things that would be better, but they knew it was pointless to argue, so they simply shrugged.

"Well, my dears, we simply must go," said Mrs. Rockman. "Those Cherry-Cheese SPAMcakes won't cook themselves! Wish us luck!"

Mr. and Mrs. Rockman were on their way to the International SPAMathon in Cheekville, Pennsylvania. The Rockmans loved SPAM, that somewhat pickled, highly pink, and frighteningly brick-shaped canned meat substance used by the army in World War II as food for soldiers and/or construction material and/or a convenient object to stuff in a cannon if needed.

Every summer, Mr. and Mrs. Rockman competed in the International SPAMathon Dessert Competition. And lost. Until last year, when Mrs. Rockman's Funky-Chunky-Chocolate SPAM Pudding captured the judges' hearts and intestinal tracts. The Rockmans were crowned SPAM King and SPAM Queen and invited back this year to defend their crowns.

Unlike their parents, Joules and Kevin did not love SPAM festivals. They thought SPAM was all right, but their parents' recipes were all wrong. So very, *very* wrong. Joules and Kevin had jumped at the chance to go to camp instead of this year's Festival of Chunky Funkiness, as they called it. What could be better than a week of swimming and hiking and eating marshmallows? But as they stood in the weeds and looked past the crumbling stone arch into the dark forest of Camp Whatsitooya, they had second thoughts.

And third thoughts.

And fourth thoughts.

"But what if something goes wrong?" asked Kevin.

"What could possibly go wrong?" asked Mrs. Rockman, blowing them a kiss as Mr. Rockman hit the gas. The squeal of tires echoed through the trees like the cry of a wounded cat.

"Famous Last Words," said Joules as she watched the family van grow smaller and smaller in the distance.

"Yep," said Kevin.

"You know what that means," said Joules.

"Yep," said Kevin.

"I hate Famous Last Words," said Joules.

"Yep," said Kevin.

Joules and Kevin Rockman shouldered their gear and headed through the crumbling stone arch into the deep woods of Camp Whatsitooya.

Chapter 7

The Rockman twins knew a lot about Famous Last Words. They had heard many of them while watching old movies on the *Late, Late, Late Creepy Show for Insomniacs* every Saturday night while their parents experimented with new recipes for SPAMalicious desserts.

As is often the case with children whose parents are obsessed with SPAM-based cooking competitions, Joules and Kevin were not what you would call "highly supervised" children. As a result, the Rockman twins had seen far more movies than most eleven-year-olds.

Remarkably, for not highly supervised children, Joules and Kevin were very responsible. They learned to cook at a young age. (Right after they learned that SPAM was not a good ingredient in pancakes or pudding or milk shakes.) They learned to clean house. (Right after they found SPAM cubes marinating in prune juice in the bathroom sink.) And they learned that sometimes adults—even the ones who love you—don't listen very well when they are thinking about something else. Especially SPAM.

Perhaps it was inevitable that Mr. and Mrs. Rockman would become obsessed with SPAM and SPAM recipes. They were scientists, after all. Mr. Rockman was a chemist and Mrs. Rockman a physicist. They were fascinated by SPAM's unique characteristics. It was a direct extension of their research into temperature and how it affects the physical properties of various substances. Which—when you think about it—is cooking.

The Rockmans were enthusiastic people and brought that enthusiasm to all their endeavors. It was this very enthusiasm, in fact, that led them to name their children Joules and Kevin. Joules was named after a famous scientist who figured out the amount of energy needed to raise the temperature of dry air one degree. Yes. Somebody actually did that. (Hey, they had to do *something* before the Internet was invented!)

It was an unusual name, and Joules liked that.

Kevin had a more complicated naming history. His intended name was "Kelvin," after a guy named Lord Kelvin who figured out how cold it has to get before everything (and that means *everything*) stops moving. For those of you smartcicles out there who also have too much time on your hands, the answer to that question is minus 273 degrees Celsius, which equals are-you-crazy?-I'm-not-going-out-in-that-kind-of-weather-it-will-freeze-my-digits-off degrees Fahrenheit.

Being named "Kelvin" after a guy who spent his time freezing things would have been a wedgie-maker for sure. Luckily for Kevin, the registration nurse at his birth sneezed while filling out the paperwork. Thus the name that showed up on his birth certificate was Kevin and thus it remains.

Joules and Kevin were happy with their names. They were good names. And most important, they were not Archimedes, Galileo, Oppenheimer, Avogadro, or Einstein. For this, they were eternally grateful.

As highly unsupervised children of SPAM-cooking scientists, Joules and Kevin Rockman developed a keen sense of awareness. They noticed things. Especially weird things. Kevin was also very organized. He liked keeping charts and records. He carried his neatly recorded observations in a notebook, which he kept with him at all times. Just in case.

Joules was not highly organized, but she recognized the value of having someone around who was. For instance, Kevin's chart "Awful Eaters and Where They Sit" helped Joules avoid many unpleasant cafeteria lunches seated next to soup slurpers, full-mouth talkers, and sloppy-joe-sauce droolers. Where Kevin liked to study a situation and make notes about it before deciding what to do next, Joules was more likely to poke a situation with a stick to see what would happen.

Though they had their own methods of approaching a situation, both understood the danger of Famous Last Words. Kevin's Chart of Famous Last Words shows this quite clearly.

Those of you who avoided reading Table 1 probably ought to be brave and read this one. It's important.

Go ahead. We'll amuse ourselves by singing while you read.

La la.

Okay, you're back. It might be a good idea for us all to stick together from here on. Of course there's nothing in this book that could possibly hurt you, and besides, if there is, it's dead already and it looks perfectly safe and it's just your imagination. . . .

KEVIN'S CHART OF FAMOUS LAST WORDS

FAMOUS LAST WORDS	SOURCE	HOW IT ENDS
"It can't escape from that."	1. *Escape of the Killer Bees* 2. *Escape of the Killer Sharks* 3. *Escape of the Killer Killers*	It escapes.
"You're safe now."	Pick a movie. Any movie.	You are definitely *not* safe.
"There's nothing in this musty, cursed tomb that could possibly hurt you."	*Curse of the Musty Tomb*	Hey! What do you know? There *is* something in the musty, cursed tomb, and it can so completely hurt you. Why are you still standing there? Run!
"Why, there's no such thing as a fill-in-the-blank."	*Attack of the fill-in-the-blank, Revenge of the fill-in-the-blank, Night of the Living fill-in-the-blank, My Grandma Is a fill-in-the-blank, Cooking with fill-in-the-blank, Fill-in-the-blank of the fill-in-the-blank*	Surprise! There really is a fill-in-the-blank and boy, are you gonna get it now!
"It looks perfectly safe to me."	Tom Bosco before eating the school's sloppy joe in third grade.	Don't ask.
"It's dead."	The most famous of all Famous Last Words.	What happens? You gotta be kidding! Ha ha ha ha ha!

Chapter 8

Meanwhile, at the edge of Camp Whatsitooya . . .

"I've got to stop a minute," said Joules.

She dropped her gear on the dirt track and rubbed the grooves in her shoulders where the straps of her backpack had been.

"What did Mom pack in these?" she asked.

"Lunch for tomorrow in case they don't have any SPAM at camp," said Kevin.

The family had eaten lunch hours ago, and Joules was getting hungry, but the thought of one of her mother's packed lunches drove away her appetite. Their mother always insisted on packing the twins SPAM-and-jelly sandwiches with sauce for lunch. Joules and Kevin tried to explain that sandwiches didn't need sauce.

"That's silly," said their mother. "All the power is in the sauce!"

Joules and Kevin had quickly learned to pack PB&Js in their lunches when Mom wasn't looking. If only they'd thought to do that today. Joules could really have gone for a PB&J right then.

Joules's stomach growled, but she ignored it. Once more she shouldered her pack and headed toward camp.

They reached the bend in the trail by the half-dead oak tree. Though in reality, "half-dead" was a ridiculous description since the whole tree was crawling with living things: ants, beetles, flies, and wasps. The creatures swarmed over the rotting tree in an endless frenzy. Hunting and being hunted.

Joules watched a small spotted moth settle gently next to a thick brown twig. Instantly, the "twig" lurched at the moth, seized it with its spiked legs, and bit into the fluttering insect. The moth's wings jerked once and were still as the praying mantis devoured its lunch. Joules shuddered and walked on.

Ahead, the trail twisted and vanished. Joules looked back toward the road, which was now a far-off patch of light, all but strangled by the dark trees. Something moved in the shadows near that light.

She stared at the spot, hoping that her parents had come back for them, but knowing, of course, that they were miles away, thinking about SPAM.

"What is it?" asked Kevin.

"I thought I saw something move back there," Joules said, pointing at the patch of light.

Kevin squinted toward the patch. All was still.

"It's noth—," he started, but he stopped when Joules gave him a say-it-and-I'll-put-grubworms-in-your-cereal look. As a take-charge kind of person, Joules was good for the threat. Even if they didn't have cereal in the morning, she would find the grubs.

Kevin couldn't blame Joules for giving him the stink-eye. After all, he was supposed to be the expert on Famous Last Words. Now he understood how easy it was to say things that you shouldn't when you are in an extraordinary situation. He decided to make a note of this on Kevin's Chart of Famous Last Words when they reached camp.

"Come on," he said.

They tromped down the track deeper into the darkness.

We've been walking a long time, thought Kevin, when he heard a low, grumbling, mumbling sound behind him and figured that it was Joules's stomach.

"Grmmblemrrrrmm."

Joules heard the grumbling, mumbling sound, too. She poked her stomach to see if the noise had come from there even though she knew it hadn't. She heard the grumbling sound again. It seemed to be behind her.

It's nothing, thought Joules, hoping it didn't count as Famous Last Words if you didn't say them out loud.

Chapter 9

As the twins walked farther into the woods, the air grew thicker. So did the ferns that swelled up from the forest floor, reaching green fingers into the still air. They were as high as Kevin's chest, and he wondered if wild animals were hiding in the ferns, watching. . . . He could almost feel their stares.

He shuddered.

Get a grip, he thought. You're acting like Annoying Movie Character Number 1.

Annoying Movie Character Number 1 is the first person in a movie to say something stupid like, "I feel like someone's watching me." This is almost always followed by someone saying Famous Last Words like, "It's nothing" or "Don't be a baby" or "It's just your imagination." Which is—of course—followed by Annoying Movie Character Number 1 being eaten by the thing that is actually watching them. On the upside, Annoying Movie Character Number 1s are well-known for their fabulous screams.

Kevin was pretty sure he had a fabulous scream, based on his reaction to the raspberry SPAM birthday cake his mom had made the twins when they turned seven. At the moment, though, he wasn't interested in showing off his fabulous scream. Instead, he made a mental note to start a new chart once they reached camp. He would call it a Field Guide to Annoying Movie Characters and it would help him remember not to act like one.

Now the trail dwindled from a double track into a single one. It went on a few feet, then stopped at an enormous fallen log.

It was the end of the road.

"This is so wrong," said Joules, throwing her backpack down in disgust.

Kevin dropped his pack and sat on the damp log. He thumped at one of the tiny mushrooms clinging to the soft wood. On the third thump, the mushroom flew into the air and disappeared in the giant ferns. Something rustled in the undergrowth.

"Grmmblemrrrrmm."

Kevin thumped another mushroom into the ferns. Again there was a rustling noise.

"Grmmblemrrrrmm."

Joules and Kevin looked at each other.

"What is it?" Joules whispered.

"I don't know," whispered Kevin.

"Go find out," Joules said.

"I have a better plan," said Kevin. "You do it."

"Wimp," said Joules.

Like most people who poked new situations with a stick, Joules was very good at finding sticks when she needed them. She picked up a stick and tiptoed toward the grumbling noise.

"Grmmblemrrrrmm."

She jabbed the stick into the ferns.

Floosh! A fluffy white bunny about the size of a small dog bolted out and bounced off Kevin's leg. Its tail was singed and blackened.

"Aaah!!!" Kevin yelled and fell back into the ferns, startling two more large bunnies with blackened rumps. They bolted after the first one and disappeared into the foliage.

Joules doubled over with laughter. "You dork!"

"Not funny," Kevin said. He pulled on his pack and tromped off through the woods.

"Wanna bet?" yelled Joules.

She pulled on her backpack and hiked after him. Had

she not been laughing so hard, she might have remembered a few basic facts of nature. Namely, that:

A. Rabbits don't grumble.

B. Rabbits don't have blackened rumps or tails.

C. Rabbits are almost never the size of a small dog. And we're not talking one of those annoying, tiny nervous-wreck "dogs" that equally annoying famous people carry in purses. We're talking the size of a real dog that's small but is going to get bigger. (Possibly much bigger.)

Had Joules not been laughing so hard, she might also have noticed the breeze that blew through the forest and rustled the tall ferns, revealing—for just a heartbeat—eyes. Six of them, to be exact. All of them swirly.

Chapter 10

Kevin and Joules hiked for what seemed like forever with no sign of a camp. They stopped by an outcropping of boulders.

Kevin set his pack on a boulder.

"This stinks," he said.

"Sure does," said Joules, dropping her pack and leaning against the rocks.

"This really, really stinks," said Kevin.

"You already said that," said Joules.

"No. I mean it *really stinks*! What's so smelly?" Kevin said.

Joules sniffed. A strange mix of rotten eggs and dead rodents filled the air.

"Oh, yeah!" Joules cried. "Lake Whatsosmelly!"

She clambered up the boulders.

"Wahoo!" she yelled from the top. "We are here!"

Kevin climbed up, too, and looked out over the sparkling waters of Lake Whatsosmelly. A canoe peacefully glided across the calm surface. On the shore stood a cluster of small tents and two large ones. A group of campers hiked up the shoreline. In the clearing near the tents, four kids and a woman with a tall beehive hairdo worked on some kind of craft project at a picnic table.

A banner stretched above the tents:

"Camp Whatsitooya. Home Sweet Camp."

A Very Brief History of Camp Whatsitooya on the Shores of Lake Whatsosmelly

Camp Whatsitooya was established in 1805 by the explorer Rodney K. Whifflesniff and his friend and bean enthusiast Benny "Beans" Malone. Following the advice of his mother, who famously invented the phrase "Get off the couch already," Whifflesniff set out to discover the elusive Northeast Passage. (Whifflesniff briefly considered seeking the elusive Northwest Passage, but honestly, it seemed kind of far and it was almost dinner and what was the big deal about the West anyhow and . . .)

On the shores of a pleasant lake, the duo paused for a medley of baked beans, boiled beans, and burned beans. (Beans Malone, while noted for his enthusiastic embrace of beans, was not known for his skill at cooking them.) Unbeknownst to the duo, the rocks on which they dined vented fumes from an underground sulfur pit (and place where small rodents liked to die). Whifflesniff sniffed the air, glared at Beans Malone, and commented, "Whatsosmelly?" Malone turned bright red, gave an embarrassed little cough, then pretended not to know what could possibly make a smell like that and said, "Whatsitooya? Let's camp."

Note that Whifflesniff and Malone's attempt to discover the Northeast Passage ended with the discovery of Boston. Population 200,000. Thrilled to learn that they existed, the citizens of Boston elected Whifflesniff as mayor and adopted Malone's bean medley as the city's favorite food to offer tourists so the locals could eat all the lobster. To this day, Boston baked beans are "enjoyed" by millions of tourists each year.

Following the establishment of Camp Whatsitooya, some historical things happened, followed by some other things that happened, and then time passed and probably some other things happened, too. All of them were boring.

Chapter 11

It was early evening. Joules and Kevin arrived in camp just as the dinner bell rang. Campers streamed into a large tent at the edge of the clearing. A sign hung above the door with the words "Mess Tent" crossed out and replaced by "Café du Lac."

The woman in the beehive hairdo walked up to the twins.

"Oh, lovely!" she said. "You must be the Rockmans. We expected you ages ago. I'm Ms. Jones, the owner and head counselor here at camp."

"We got lost," said Joules.

"Wonderful!" exclaimed Ms. Jones. "You've had a chance to explore the grounds and enjoy our beautiful scenery here at Camp Whatsitooya. I hope you got to experience the Aroma Rocks."

"The stinky boulders?" asked Kevin.

"Yes indeed!" said Ms. Jones. "They are one of our most famous features. People hike for miles just to avoid them. Well, you must be starving. Why don't you drop your gear in here." She pointed to one of the small tents. "Then come dine with us at Café du Lac. It's steak night. Tube steaks! All the campers just love them, and we just love our campers! Always the best at Camp Whatsitooya!"

"I think she means hot dogs," whispered Kevin.

"Works for me!" said Joules, tossing her pack into the tent and running to join the other campers in the mess tent.

"Wait for me!" yelled Kevin, dropping his pack and running after her.

Café du Lac was surprisingly large. It held four large picnic tables and was lit by camp lanterns that hung from the ceiling. Three boys sat at one table. At the end of the tent was a camp kitchen where three girls with ponytails and pink T-shirts were busy serving the other campers. In a corner, behind the stack of trays, was a large stack of boxes marked "marshmallows." Oh, yeah!

Joules and Kevin got in line for hot dogs behind a skinny, freckled boy with rumpled reddish hair, droopy socks, and a wrinkled T-shirt.

"You picked the right day to come to camp!" said the boy. "Tube steaks are the best! I never get to have them at home because my mom says that cylinder-shaped foods are unnatural and can cause goiters. I'm not sure what goiters are, but I don't want them. I don't think I'll write Mom about the tube steaks. Do you think I should write Mom about the tube steaks? I'm Nelson."

"Uh . . . ," said Joules.

"Well . . . ," said Kevin.

"I didn't think so," said Nelson. "I'll tell her about the potato chips. They're kind of oval. Who are you?"

Joules and Kevin introduced themselves.

"Twins are cool," said Nelson. "I'm not twins. There's only one of me. Mom says that there could never be anyone else like me. I think she's right. 'Cause then there would be two of me."

"Wow," said Joules.

The three girls handed Nelson his tray of food, which included a hot dog, chips, some homemade baked beans, and salad. He carried his tray to an empty picnic table by the door and sat down.

"You can sit by me!" he called to the twins.

"Great," whispered Kevin.

The girls serving dinner looked up. Even though their faces looked nothing alike, the three girls seemed identical. Or more accurately—they seemed interchangeable. They wore matching pink shirts and had their hair pulled back in pink sparkly scrunchies. Even their pink hiking boots were decorated with matching hearts and stars.

"Hi," said Kevin. "I'm Kevin and this is Joules."

"I'm SmellyCat," said the girls, and they giggled.

Actually, they said, "I'm Sam. I'm Ellie. I'm Cat."

Unfortunately, they all said it at the same time, and it sounded like *SamEllieCat*, which sounded just like *SmellyCat* to Kevin and Joules. The twins thought about asking them to repeat their names, but frankly it took more energy than they could muster after a long day of being lost and nearly starving to death.

"Thanks for the tube steaks," said Joules.

The twins took their trays and lemonade to Nelson's table and sat down. SmellyCat loaded up their trays and sat at another table.

The tent buzzed with the chatter of happy campers retelling the tales of the day's adventures. The smell of baked beans and tube steaks, tent canvas and wood smoke filled the air. For the first time all day, Joules and Kevin Rockman relaxed. Camp Whatsitooya looked just like camp should. Lots of fun. Lots of food. And none of it brick-shaped. Things were going to be fine. Just fine.

Joules and Kevin raised their glasses of lemonade in a silent toast and took a sip.

Camp Whatsitooya. Home Sweet Camp.

Chapter 12

Perhaps you are wondering what has happened since we left the Fluffs on their smoldering marshmallow planet thinking, "Evacuate!!!!"

Perhaps you are not.

If not, what are you doing? Really. This is an interesting topic. What could you possibly be doing that is more interesting than this? Are you cleaning your room? Because really, that's not at all interesting. Are you playing a video game? Are you wishing you had a chocolate triple-dip ice-cream cone?

Or maybe a *mint* chocolate chip dip cone.

Mmmmmm. Hold that thought—

Chapter 13

Wow. That was so delicious. So where were we? Oh, yes . . .

When last we left our alien friends (and by "friends," we mean evil alien rabbits capable of wiping out half the human race with their fangs and floppy ears), their marshmallow planet was in peril.

Here's an instant replay:

"EVACUATE!" thought Floopsy.

"EVACUATE!" thought Moopsy.

"BURP!" thought Cottonswab.

Here's what happened next:

"Go get in that rocket that landed on the other side of the planet a few years back," thought Cottonswab.

"Says who?" thought Moopsy and Floopsy. "What makes you the boss around here?"

"BURP!" thought Cottonswab.

"Aye-aye, commander!" thought Moopsy and Floopsy.

"I like the sound of that!" thought Commander Cottonswab.

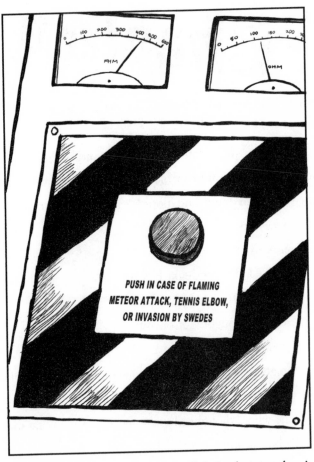

The Fluffs rounded the corner of their planet and arrived
at an aging rocket. The rocket had arrived several years before
and sent out small robotic rovers that drove over the planet
gathering pictures via their cameras and small dirt samples

via their pinchy-grabby robot arms. The rovers were not dangerous. But they tasted pretty good with chocolate sauce.

The Fluffs boarded the aging rocket.

"Do you guys know how to fly this thing?" thought Floopsy.

"How hard can it be?" thought Moopsy. "Push some buttons. That one looks big."

"Push in case of Swedes?" thought Commander Cottonswab. "They sound tasty. Let's go."

Commander Cottonswab pushed the large red button.

The rocket shook and rumbled. The rocket fuel tanks ignited with a deafening roar. (For those of you gifted at sound effects, insert an extremely loud rocket blast kind of roar here.)

Then—*SHWOOOOOOOOOOSH!!!!!!!!!*

The rocket lifted into the air, flames torching the fluffy marshmallow surface of the planet, which burned orange, then blue, and finally crumbled into a powdery black ash and shattered into the nothingness of space.

The Planet of the Fluffs was no more.

"Wow," thought Floopsy.

"Wow," thought Moopsy.

"Swedes," thought Commander Cottonswab. "Yum."

Chapter 14

After dinner, Kevin and Joules Rockman returned to their tiny tent and flopped onto their cots, which were surprisingly comfortable. The twins had not realized how tired they were, but within moments, they were fast asleep.

It was dark outside when Kevin woke and realized that he needed to use the bathroom. He also realized that he had no idea where the bathroom was. He shook Joules by the shoulder.

"Wake up," he said. "I need to find the bathroom."

"Spa," Joules grumbled. She flopped over on her cot and started snoring. "Thanks bunches," muttered Kevin.

He pulled a flashlight out of his backpack, slid into his sneakers, and slipped out of the tent. The other campers were asleep in the surrounding tents, and the camp was dark and silent. Well, not *exactly* silent. There were no people noises, but the forest was like a soundtrack from *Attack of the Jungle Monsters of Death*. Crickets and frogs and—quite possibly—werewolves and human-sized Gila monsters creaked and croaked and howled and breathed heavily in the trees. Other creatures, Kevin was sure, were waiting silently for their chance to chew his kneecaps off.

Wandering aimlessly in the dark in a strange place was at the top of Kevin's list—and yes, Kevin kept an actual list in his notebook—of things to avoid. Kevin was not a fan of the dark. In fact, though he would not admit it, the dark was one of the reasons Kevin Rockman liked plans so much. As a young kid, he had been scared of the dark. He overcame his fear by drawing and memorizing maps of his room so he could remember where to run in case of ghost attack or bedbug invasion. Plans comforted Kevin.

What did not comfort Kevin was stepping into the darkness of Camp Whatsitooya without knowing where he was going. He could kick himself for not figuring it out earlier. He shined his flashlight over the tents and noticed a beaten path between two of them. Kevin followed it past the dining tent to the edge of the clearing.

This can't be right, he thought.

He was about to turn around when his flashlight beam hit a small, sparkly sign with an arrow and the word "SPA" printed on it. Kevin followed the trail into the woods. As the forest sounds grew louder and louder, Kevin added more creatures to the list of possible noisemakers: anacondas, zombies, and termites. Each had an evil way of killing a person. Kevin tried to figure out which would be the best way to go. He decided that being eaten by the giant snake would be best. At least if he was eaten by an anaconda, Joules would see the Kevin-shaped snake happily sunning itself (while digesting its midnight snack) on the trail to the spa and figure out what had happened to him.

Kevin walked faster. At last, the path broadened in front of a small rickety building. It was the outhouse—a.k.a. the spa—from the brochure. It was old and rickety, but Kevin had never been happier to find a place.

There were two entrances to the building. A small, crooked sign hung over the left entrance. It was an icon of a figure wearing a skirt. The other had no sign at all. Since he was neither a girl nor a boy wearing a kilt, Kevin opted for the second entrance. He pulled open the door and walked inside.

Here's a thought. Why don't we give Kevin some privacy? We could build a campfire and sing some songs and tell some spooky stories and eat some s'mores. Did anyone bring marshmallows?

No? C'mon folks! We're at a camp!

Okay. Well, never mind.

Besides, he shouldn't be in there that much longer. Right?

. . . .
. . . .
. . . .
. . . .
. . . .
. . . .
. . . .
. . . .
. . . .

. . . . la la la la. Boy, this is taking a long time. . . .
. . . .
. . . .
. . . .
. . . .
. . . .

. . . . Any time now, Kevin. . . . .
. . . .
. . . .
. . . .
. . . .
. . . .

. . . . Nice evening, isn't it? . . . .

. . . .

. . . .

. . . .

. . . . Read any good books lately? . . . .

. . . .

. . . .

. . . .

. . . .

. . . .

46 . . . .

. . . .

. . . .

On the other hand, he could be in there all night. So why don't we chat a little. This would be a great time to clear up any questions you might have so far.

What? Oh, sure. Now he's ready. No time for questions. But here are some answers just in case you have questions later:

1. The blue-footed goonie bird

2. May 27, 1992

3. Causes an unsightly rash and swelling

Meanwhile, back to our story . . .

—reaching for the door to leave the spa, Kevin heard rustling outside and a strange chomping noise.

RUSTLE . . . RUSTLE . . .
RUSTLE . . . CHOMP . . .
CHOMP . . . CHOMP . . .

Kevin froze. The sounds grew closer and closer until they were just outside the screen door.

RUSTLE . . . RUSTLE . . .
RUSTLE . . . CHOMP . . .
CHOMP . . . CHOMP . . .

Kevin held his breath. He couldn't see what was making the noise, but he could tell by the sounds that it was big. Very, very big. And, frankly, it didn't sound very nice. Kevin was about to duck back into a stall when the sound stopped. The rustling chomping thing chomped and rustled off into the woods behind the spa and was gone. Kevin heard a new sound and saw a flashlight beam in the dark. Someone was stumbling down the path toward the spa.

"Kevin!?"

It was Joules.

"Here!" he called.

"What's taking you so long?" she asked.

"Just enjoying the spa," said Kevin. "What do you think?"

"Geez," said Joules. "Way to trash the joint."

"What are you talking about?" asked Kevin.

Joules pointed her flashlight on the ground outside the door, where a dozen shredded candy wrappers littered the path.

"It wasn't me," said Kevin. "There was something out here. Something big and noisy that went **RUSTLE . . . RUSTLE . . . RUSTLE . . . CHOMP . . . CHOMP . . . CHOMP.** Besides, where would I get candy this time of night?"

"Whatever," said Joules. "It was probably one of the other campers."

"I don't know," said Kevin. "It sounded pretty weird for a camper."

"What else would hang out by the spa eating candy in the middle of the night?" she asked. "Aliens?"

Chapter 15

And speaking of aliens . . .

Let's take a moment to fill in some gaps about the Fluffs and what happened after they boarded the rocket on the far side of their planet and pushed the comically large red button to be used in case of flaming meteor attack, tennis elbow, or invasion by Swedes.

Pushing this button initiated the Unexpected Return Protocol (URP). The URP in the rocket's computer triggered a homing beacon designed to guide the rocket back to its starting point on planet Earth.

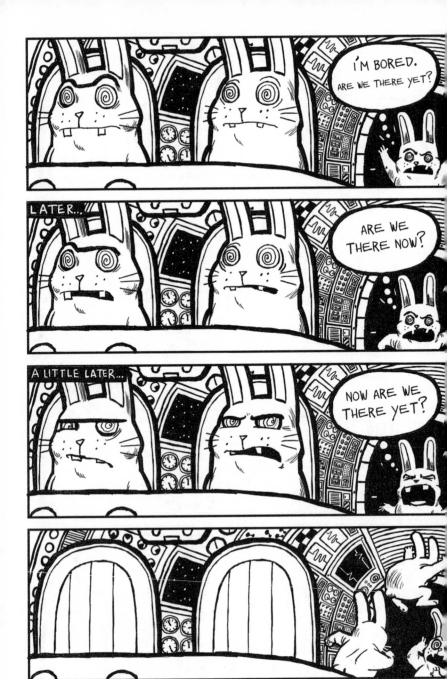

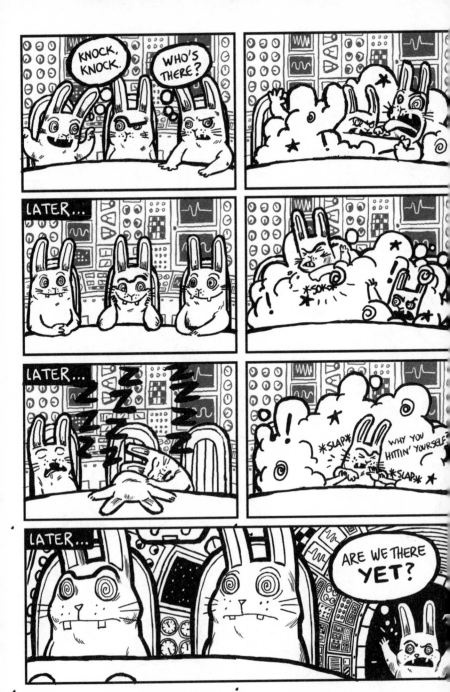

The Fluffs traveled farther and farther from the Starburst at the center of their galaxy. The Starburst whose sweet sugary goodness provided them energy and carried the telepathic waves that allowed them to communicate. As the distance from their home grew, the Fluffs shrank. And so did their telepathic ability.

CRASH!

....sssssssss...

Small, unable to communicate accurately, and craving something sugary, the three shrunken Fluffs hopped off to find a snack. Preferably something very, very sweet. And Swedish.

Chapter 16

Joules and Kevin woke early the next morning and breathed in the pine needle and campfire–scented summer air. A faint aroma of frying bacon drifted from Café du Lac.

Ahhhh, camp.

They unpacked their bags, which they had dumped on the floor of the tent the night before. Joules tossed the plastic tubs of sauce and sandwiches under her cot, and they headed to the dining tent, where the other campers were already eating.

There were ten kids at Camp Whatsitooya, including the twins. Joules recognized SmellyCat and Nelson from the day before. SmellyCat sat with a new girl with braids. Nelson sat with three younger boys. He waved wildly at Joules, who ignored him.

Ms. Jones and two men were cooking in the camp kitchen. One was a short, nervous-looking middle-aged man with very pointy hair and a long white lab coat. He also wore long rubber gloves and lab goggles. He cautiously poked at the bacon with a long pair of tongs and ducked at each pop and snap of grease on the griddle.

The other man was extremely handsome and in his early twenties. He was tall and tanned with his dark hair pulled into a ponytail. He wore a "Surfers get Board" T-shirt, long surf shorts, and flip-flops. He was flipping pancakes and jamming to his iPod, but smiled when he saw the twins.

The smell of the pancakes and bacon filled the tent with the most delicious aroma. This was heaven.

"Good morning, campers. This is Counselor Blech," said Ms. Jones, gesturing toward the pointy-haired man as he cautiously prodded a piece of bacon. "And that's Counselor Jammer." She waved her hand at the pancake-flipper. "Welcome to Café du Lac," she continued. "After breakfast, you're on my team for crafts, then boating with Counselor Jammer."

"All right, dudes!" said the surfer chef, who gave them the "hang ten" sign.

"Cool," said Kevin, grabbing a plate of food and heading over to sit by Nelson.

Joules grabbed a plate and headed to the table with SmellyCat and the girl with braids. SmellyCat were chattering together and seemed to have developed a whole language of their own that involved all the girls talking at once, followed by giggling and occasional snorting. It was a kind of gigglesnort dialect.

The girl in braids had a sparkling smile. Literally. She had two flakes of silver glitter stuck to her front tooth. Joules thought about saying something to her, but the girl also had flecks of glitter stuck to her hair. Joules smiled and started eating. The girl smiled back. Sparkle. Sparkle.

"Hi. I'm Mitzy," she said, though Joules was too distracted by the glitter to pay attention. All Joules could think was, Sparkletooth. Sparkletooth.

"I heard you are coming to do crafts after breakfast. That's so exciting. Today I get to be Junior Craft Leader! Some of the kids do boating first and then do crafts, but that's no fun. It's always best to start the day with crafts. Crafts are the best part of camp. I could do crafts all day. I think blah blah crafts blah blah crafts—"

Sparkletooth . . . Sparkletooth . . . At this point, Joules stopped listening entirely and ate her breakfast. She went back for seconds and was almost done eating when Sparkletooth finished talking.

"—blah blah crafts. Won't that be awesome?"

She let out a dreamy kind of sigh.

SmellyCat sighed, too, then they said something in GiggleSnort that sounded like "GlitGlueFun," followed by a round of giggles and snorts. Clearly, the four girls shared a love of all things sweet, glittery, and crafty. Joules groaned. She hated crafts. Next to watching golf on TV, there was nothing more boring than trying to glue shiny gluey things to other shiny gluey things so you could take them home to put in a massive pile of shiny gluey things you made last year and the year before and will never ever ever *ever* use in a million years. Crafts with Popsicle sticks were the worst. What was the point of a Popsicle stick without the Popsicle?

Joules finished eating and was about to leave when SmellyCat said, "CanTentThief!"

"No way!" said Sparkletooth. "Did they find out who did it?"

"What?" asked Joules.

"StoleLotsCan," said SmellyCat, and they shot a glance at Kevin.

"Wow!" said Sparkletooth.

"What???" asked Joules.

"Someone stole candy from Avery's tent last night and took it up by the spa and ate it all and left the wrappers all over the place and now Avery is in trouble because you're not supposed to keep candy in your tent because of the wild animals around at night. The counselors are saying a raccoon ate it, but who knows really? Maybe it's a robber. That kid looks sort of suspicious."

"They said all that?" asked Joules. "Hey wait! Do they mean *that* kid??? Kevin didn't do it. He found all the trash on the ground."

SmellyCat glanced knowingly at one another and Sparkletooth.

"Sure."

And somehow, that one word said it all.

Chapter 17

The original Camp Whatsitooya was established in the 1940s as a vacation spot for homesick Norwegians, but failed when the Norwegians remembered that Norway, while cold, had actual plumbing. The homesick Norwegians returned to their homeland, which permanently cured their homesickness but did little for Camp Whatsitooya's finances.

Ms. Jones purchased the camp a few months before Joules and Kevin arrived. She had dreams of transforming it into a crafting resort and amusement park for all ages—just like Disneyland, but with more Styrofoam balls and fewer talking rodents. Ms. Jones hoped that Craftland would become a vacation destination for glue-gun gurus everywhere. For now, it was two picnic tables covered in craft supplies beneath an elm tree on the shore of Lake Whatsosmelly.

At 9:30, Kevin and Joules arrived at the tables beneath the hand-painted sign: "Craftland—Creating Smiles One Project at a Time."

SmellyCat sat at a table chatting and giggling. Nelson plopped down on the seat next to Kevin.

"I heard you're a suspect in the Case of the Missing Candy," Nelson said to Kevin.

"It's not a case and I'm not a suspect," said Kevin.

"That's what I told the other kids," said Nelson. "I said you're a lot nicer than most thieves."

"Well, you're a lot nicer than most kids I stuff into garbage cans," said Joules, though she had never actually stuffed anyone into a garbage can. (The closest she had ever come was "helping" a bully in fourth grade explore the inside of his gym locker.)

"You think so?" asked Nelson. "Mom says going to camp every summer has helped my interpersonal skills a lot."

"It shows," said Kevin, shooting a look at Joules.

Nelson beamed.

"I know!" he said. "I always make a lot of friends, and everyone is really excited at the end of summer when I say good-bye and promise to write them. And I do, too. But they aren't very good at writing back. I don't know why. What do you think?"

"No idea," said Joules and Kevin at the same time.

Three younger boys arrived and sat at the opposite end

of the twins' table. They whispered to one another and looked nervously at Kevin.

"That's Avery and his friends Jack and Eric," Nelson said to Kevin. "They think you're going to beat them up for their candy."

"What?" asked Kevin. "I wouldn't do that! Hey, kid! I didn't take your candy."

Kevin smiled his friendliest smile, but the younger boys looked frightened. They pretended to be fascinated by a pill bug walking across the table.

"Tell them, Joules," said Kevin.

She did not answer. Joules was too busy gawking at Ms. Jones, who was walking toward Craftland with Sparkletooth. The two wore matching pink safari outfits with rhinestone buttons, beaded collars, and glittery hiking boots. Glue guns were slung to their hips like a gunslinger's six-shooters. Scissors, pliers, Styrofoam balls, glue sticks, fringe, and vials of glitter were jammed in their tool belts.

"Wonderful!" cooed Ms. Jones. "So pleased that all of you could come to Craftland to enjoy a morning of personal growth and well-being through glitter. Mitzy will be Junior Craft Leader today, and I know she is very excited about it."

Sparkletooth smiled her shiniest smile ever.

"I am overjoyed," she said. "Ever since my parents died in that unfortunate toast accident, it has been my greatest dream to have a new family and lovely friends just like you. And to bring happiness to the world through glitter! This is a dream come true."

Sparkle. Sparkle.

"Awwwww," said SmellyCat, jumping up and hugging Sparkletooth in a blob of pink glittery giggles.

"I think I'm going to be nauseous," whispered Joules.

Kevin nodded.

"That's probably from all the bacon you ate," whispered Nelson. "Mom says that too much bacon can make your tail curly. I don't think that would be good, do you?"

Joules and Kevin just shook their heads. It was going to be a long morning.

Chapter 18

After what seemed like hours of hugging and gigglesnorting, craft class finally began.

"Today we're making lanyards," said Ms. Jones. "You can't get too many of those."

Nelson whispered to Kevin, "Actually, you can. I have seventeen at home, and I'm pretty sure that's enough. Though maybe one more won't hurt. What do you think?"

Perhaps you have not been to camp and are asking yourself, "What is a lanyard?" or "Why would I need a lanyard?" or, more important, "What's for lunch?"

Here are the answers:

1. A lanyard is a fancy string for carrying things like keys around your neck.
2. Lanyards are useful because it's always fun to wear things around your neck so they can get caught on branches while you hike. And . . .
3. We just had breakfast. Try to focus already!

Ms. Jones and Mitzy distributed bundles of twine and plastic bags of beads and feathers to the campers, who knotted and threaded and twisted the twine into lanyards, then glued feathers to them.

Kevin actually liked crafts. The slow pace and attention to detail suited him. He had spent many hours creating detailed maps and models and always found the process of creating things relaxing. Joules, on the other hand, hated it. It bored and annoyed her.

The longer she sat trying to thread her twine through the beads, the crankier she got. The third time she trapped her finger in a knot of twine, she'd had enough.

"I need to visit the spa," she said, and got up from the picnic table.

"Of course, dear!" said Ms. Jones. "Enjoy your scenic stroll to our historically significant facilities, and hurry back to join us. You won't want to miss any of the fun. We're going to learn all about the history of lanyards!"

"I'll rush right back," said Joules, by which she meant, "I'll rush right back to my tent and take a nap, then pretend I got lost when you ask where I was for two hours."

Joules left Craftland and headed toward the spa. Just as she passed the Café du Lac, she heard a series of thumps and a loud **RUSTLE . . . RUSTLE . . . RUSTLE . . . CHOMP . . . CHOMP . . . CHOMP** inside. She reached for the door.

CRASH!!! BAM!!! RIP!!!!!!

Joules stepped into the unlit tent and waited for her eyes to adjust to the darkness. For just one instant, she saw a white bear-sized creature squeeze through a rip in the tent canvas. She ran after it and tripped over a pile of pots and pans strewn across the floor. She fell face-first onto something sticky. And that's when someone turned on the light.

Chapter 19

"Girl dude!" said Jammer. "Why are you all—like— bodysurfing in the syrup? That's so not cool."

Joules was lying in a giant puddle of pancake syrup.

At that moment, the door opened and Ms. Jones came in, followed by the campers from Craftland.

Ms. Jones gasped.

"What on Earth did you do?" she asked.

"It wasn't me!" said Joules. "There was a big hairy thing and it ripped the tent and went that way. I think it was a bear."

She pointed at the gash in the canvas, but Ms. Jones didn't even look. She was livid. She grabbed her glue guns like a cowboy with itchy trigger fingers.

"Miss Rockman. Go to the spa and get cleaned up, then return to your tent while I contact your parents."

"But—," said Joules. "I—"

"Now!" said Ms. Jones.

Joules peeled herself out of the sticky puddle as Sparkletooth cried, "Ms. Jones. She ate all the marshmallows!"

Indeed, the crates of marshmallows were gone. The only sign of them was a lone marshmallow stuck in the puddle of syrup on the floor.

Chapter 20

Joules sat on her cot, poking the tent canvas with a stick she had found on the way back from the spa. It had taken her forever to get cleaned up. Being drenched in syrup was bad enough, but on the way to the spa, she had tripped on a root and fallen into a pile of pine needles. By the time she reached the showers, she looked like a porcupine and smelled like a pancake.

Camp was definitely not turning out as she had planned. But the worst part was knowing that Ms. Jones was calling her parents. Joules was now doomed to spend the rest of the week at the Festival of Chunky Funkiness for a crime she hadn't committed. The thought of it made her blood boil, and she jabbed harder at the tent roof.

"Hey! You'll poke a hole in it, and we'll get wet if it rains!" said Kevin.

He and Nelson stuck their heads into the tent.

"Nelson saw some big footprints outside the mess tent and found these stuck on a tree at the edge of the woods by Craftland," said Kevin, holding a small clump of short white hairs. "We tried to follow the trail, but lost it in the ferns. Whatever ripped that tent was big and fast."

"And hungry," said Nelson. "That was a lot of marsh-mallows. It's a real mystery! I love mysteries. Mom says I could grow up to be a great detective since I like to watch mysteries on TV so much. Almost as much as I like to watch shows about plumbing. I think they are really interesting. What do you thi—"

"Shhhh," said Kevin. "Here comes the Craft Queen. Let's get out of here."

"Chickens!" yelled Joules as Kevin and Nelson ran off to the canoe launch.

A moment later, Ms. Jones arrived at the tent and asked Joules to step outside.

"I am extremely disappointed in your behavior, Miss Rockman," she said. "I have never witnessed such disregard for crafting and the enjoyment of other crafters."

"But—" said Joules.

Ms. Jones raised her well-manicured hand to stop Joules from speaking.

"We have attempted to contact your parents, but they are not answering their phone at the moment," said Ms. Jones.

Hurray for International SPAMathons, thought Joules.

"We shall keep trying to reach your parents," said Ms. Jones. "Until then, I am sad to say that you are not to participate in any more crafting activities at Camp Whatsitooya."

"Awwww," said Joules, trying very hard to look disappointed.

Ms. Jones continued.

"I know this is hard for you," she said. "And it saddens me deeply because I know the joys of attaining personal enlightenment through the crafts. Still, I cannot put the happiness of others aside for the needs of one who has shown utter disdain for glitter."

"You mean I can't finish my lanyard?" asked Joules. "Well, I'll stick around here and try to do better."

She made a sad little "sorry" face.

"See that you do," said Ms. Jones, walking away from the tent.

Joules lay back on her cot. Three seconds later, she got up and walked around the tent three times, tapping the canvas with her stick as she walked.

"That ought to count as sticking around," she said to herself.

Joules Rockman headed into the woods to solve a mystery. A big mystery with white fur and a taste for marshmallows.

Chapter 21

Nelson had chores to do at Café du Lac, so Kevin headed to the canoe launch alone. Avery, Sparkletooth, and SmellyCat were at the launch watching Jammer polish a blue-and-white surfboard. He was telling them about Hawaii, where they had the best surf in the world.

Working at Camp Whatsitooya had not been Jammer's original plan. He had been a little confused about the distance from Atlantic City to Hawaii. After all, it was only four inches on the map he kept in his wallet. How long could that take? As it turns out, a lot more than a day when you are riding a bike and trying to haul your surfboard. Jammer stopped to work at Camp Whatsitooya for a few weeks to earn some cash to buy a plane ticket or at least a bigger bicycle.

"Dudes," said Jammer. "Like, welcome. This is Canoeing 101, and we're going to have some fun. Okay, so—like—everybody get in a canoe and—like—canoe. Yeah. Hang ten!"

It was the quickest lesson Kevin had ever had for anything, and he didn't like it. He liked lessons that included details and planned for problems like death, destruction, locusts, and panic. He had never canoed before and really didn't know anything about boats. A little extra information might have been useful.

SmellyCat and Sparkletooth got into two canoes and paddled into the lake. The girls paddled along the shore, giggling and snorting after every stroke. Avery stood beside the third canoe and looked at Kevin with pure terror in his eyes.

"No worries, Avery dude. Just get in and paddle," said Jammer. "Surf's up!"

Jammer put in his earphones and started waxing his surfboard again, and the instruction was over.

Avery seemed as nervous as Kevin, but Kevin suspected it was for different reasons. Avery stepped into the front of the canoe and Kevin stepped into the back, shoving the canoe from the shore. They glided a few feet onto the lake and started paddling. With each stroke Kevin took, Avery paddled twice. Kevin paddled faster to keep up, which made Avery paddle even faster. Avery paddled harder and harder, as if he were trying to get away from Kevin. Every few strokes, he stole a terrified glance over his shoulder.

In minutes, they were in the middle of Lake What-sosmelly. The air was warm and breezy. It should have been pleasant gliding through the calm waters, but a distinct chill came from Avery, who sat stiffly staring straight ahead.

"Hey, look," said Kevin. "I'm really sorry somebody stole your candy, but it wasn't me."

Avery made a faint gasp and dug harder into the water with the wooden paddle. He did not answer.

"Hey," said Kevin.

"I don't have any more candy," said Avery in a panic. "But I'll give you my lunch. Just let me go!"

"Hey! I'm not going to take your candy, and I don't want your lunch. I'm not a thief! Really!" Kevin said. "It's okay."

Avery shrunk into a ball on the front seat of the canoe and said, "Go away."

Kevin pulled his paddle from the water and very gently nudged Avery's back with the handle.

"It's okay!" he said.

At the touch of the canoe paddle, Avery bolted out of his seat.

"AAAAAAAAAAHHHHHH!!!" he screamed, and jumped into the lake, sending both paddles flying in one direction and the canoe spinning in the other.

"Come back!" yelled Kevin. "Hey! You can't just jump out like that! I don't know how to canoe!"

Avery swam for the shore like a shark was after him. He was a fast swimmer, but Kevin was too dizzy from the spinning motion of the canoe to watch. The swirling twirling motion reminded him of the time the family had gone to the county fair after trying out Mrs. Rockman's new recipe for Spaco-bagos (a.k.a. SPAM Tacos with Rutabaga). After two Spaco-bagos and a couple of cotton candies, Kevin and Joules went on the Tilt-A-Whirl. This was, coincidentally, the same day Kevin discovered the wonders of motion sickness.

Now, in his twirling canoe in the middle of Lake Whatsosmelly, Kevin recognized the familiar feeling swelling up inside him. He clung, white-knuckled, to the sides of the canoe and clamped his eyes shut. That didn't work. The feeling grew stronger. He opened his eyes and tried to focus on one spot in the distance. His eyes settled on the giant elm tree at Craftland. Ms. Jones sat by herself at one of the picnic tables. Kevin spun around again. Ms. Jones was still at the table, but she was not alone. Kevin spun around again and again. With each spin, the scene on the shore unfolded like panels in a comic book, though there was nothing comical about what was happening. You can see for yourself what it looked like on the next page.

"Watch out!!!!" Kevin yelled.

He stood up in the canoe pointing wildly at the shore, where Ms. Jones was being dragged away.

"Help!" Kevin yelled to Jammer or anyone who might hear.

He meant it in a There's-a-really-weird-creature-attacking-Ms.-Jones-somebody-help-her kind of way, but it came off as more of a Help!-I-don't-know-that-it's-stupid-to-stand-up-in-a-canoe-and-this-is-going-to-end-very-badly kind of way because at that moment, Kevin Rockman pointed a little too far toward the shore. He realized this was a problem when he found himself pointing toward a largemouth bass swimming through the murky depths of Lake Whatsosmelly.

SPLASH!

Kevin tumbled down into the water but immediately bobbed back up thanks to his life jacket. Floating on his back in the middle of the lake, Kevin noticed four things:

1. It was a very pretty day, though a dark cloud in the west threatened rain.

2. Canoes drift away very fast when you are not in them but want to be.

3. Jammer was a fast runner and an even faster surfboard paddler. He would do great in Hawaii.

4. Ms. Jones was gone.

Chapter 22

After Joules left the tent, she headed toward Café du Lac, carefully ducking out of sight when Counselor Blech and a pair of campers passed by on the way to swim at the beach. Or at least that was what Joules guessed. The campers wore swimsuits and Counselor Blech wore a deep-sea diver's outfit. He carried the fishbowl-shaped helmet under his arm.

"And remember," he said, "if you see a fish, swim for your life. Don't worry about me. I'll be safe on the shore."

The campers groaned and marched on.

Joules slipped behind Café du Lac and saw the giant gash in the canvas. Someone had patched the rip with silver duct tape to keep mosquitoes from enjoying a meal while the campers enjoyed theirs. That was thoughtful.

She found the large, flat footprints in the dirt and a small clump of white fur snagged on a raspberry bramble. Another tuft of fur clung to a branch a few feet away. A trail of clues.

The trail led into the deep ferns, and Joules followed it. Bending low and constantly pushing fern fronds out of her face, she searched the ground for footprints. Eventually, the

trail led to an open stand of trees that skirted the shore of the lake. Joules looked out onto the water.

She saw three canoes in the lake and one blue-and-white surfboard on the shore. Two of the canoes were skimming the far shore, and she recognized SmellyCat and Sparkletooth in them. She could occasionally catch the faint sound of their giggles on the breeze that blew across the water and gently rustled the leaves. The third canoe paddled furiously toward the center of the lake. She recognized Avery and Kevin. Kevin had learned to canoe!

Way to go, Kev! she thought, and turned back to the trail.

She followed the prints a little farther along the shore, but they soon vanished. A deer trail veered into the deeper woods. Joules followed it, hoping it would lead her somewhere useful. Had she stayed close to the shore, she might have heard a cry for help, a very large splash, and someone calling, "Hey, dude! Don't get all—like—drowned or something. Uncool!"

Joules missed these things.

As she headed into the woods, the wind shifted and the giggling sounds were replaced by the chittering of squirrels and the occasional caw of a crow that flew from tree to tree, its golden eyes fixed on the girl following a path used only by deer and—lately—three other creatures. Strange, white, fluffy creatures with crates of marshmallows.

Chapter 23

With our heroes pursuing mysteries and awaiting rescue in a large lake, let's take a moment to enjoy these messages about our favorite products.

Bob's Life Preservers!

Floating good. Drowning Bad.

SPAM

Unnaturally square.

Unnaturally good.

Chapter 24

Joules continued through the woods along the narrow deer path. She had seen no footprints or tufts of fur for a long time and was ready to turn back. It would be dinner soon, and she was getting hungry, though she wasn't sure if she was hungry enough to face the whispers and sidelong glances from the campers at Café du Lac. Of course, she could always skip dinner. There was still the lunch with secret sauce Mom had packed, which had been ripening under her cot for a full day now.

Joules thought about it for a moment and realized that the words "lunch" and "ripening" should never be used in the same sentence. Thank goodness for Tupperware and those airtight seals! Without them, she and Kevin might have been killed by toxic fumes in their sleep. She made a mental note to pitch the lunch before it exploded or something worse. It was the kind of toxic substance that could turn into a new life form and threaten the camp and who knows what else. Joules and Kevin had seen things like this a million times on the *Late, Late, Late Creepy Show for Insomniacs,* though usually the toxic substance was the accidental result of some science experiment gone terribly awry. . . .

Joules sighed and leaned against the trunk of a large oak to rest for a moment. The brush was very thick here, and going any farther would be too much work. She was tired and stared around lazily without paying much attention to what she was seeing. After a moment, though, she realized that she was staring at a fence. A tall chain-link fence that ran behind the line of bushes. What was on the other side?

Joules was about to investigate when she heard:

RUSTLE . . . RUSTLE . . . RUSTLE . . . CHOMP . . . CHOMP . . . CHOMP. She ducked behind the oak tree and listened. The sound came closer and closer to Joules's hideout. It stopped on the other side of the tree. Joules clenched the end of her stick, took a deep breath, and jumped out of her hiding place.

"I got y—" she yelled, ready to jab whatever she found on the other side of the tree.

What she found was Ms. Jones. Joules dropped her stick.

"Uh—" she said. "Hi?"

Ms. Jones stood before her wearing a pair of dark sunglasses. She swayed oddly from side to side, her cyclone-shaped hair tilting dangerously as she swayed. She looked Joules over from head to toe as if she were sizing her up. There was something very odd about her, or more accurately, about the way she appeared to Joules. Ms. Jones was fuzzy. Not a covered-with-peach-fuzz type of fuzzy, but blurry, as if Joules had just awakened and her eyes had not yet adjusted to the light. When Ms. Jones spoke, her voice was flat and expressionless. Almost robotic.

"Are you Swedish?" she asked.

"Uh. No . . . ," Joules said slowly. "I think my family is Danish and English."

"Danish are tasty," said Ms. Jones. "English are not."

"Uh-huh," said Joules uneasily. "Um. Are you okay?"

"Yes," said Ms. Jones. "I am accessing memories. You are the Rockman female camper. You are not sweet."

"Thanks," said Joules. "I get that a lot."

"That can be corrected," said Ms. Jones. "Then you will be useful."

"Are you feeling okay, Ms. Jones?" asked Joules.

"Ms. Jones?"

The counselor tilted her head to the other side.

"That is a terrible name," she said. "Call me Commander Cotton—er—Jones. Commander Jones. That is a good name. Go away."

"Okay," said Joules.

Joules was very happy to get away from Ms.—er—Commander Jones. She was giving Joules the creeps. Joules started back toward camp, but after a few steps turned around.

"Are you sure you're okay?"

Commander Jones was gone.

Chapter 25

Kevin returned from his canoeing adventure expecting to find Joules sharpening a stick on her cot and planning her escape from Camp Whatsitooya. But the tent was empty. Perhaps she had gone back to the spa. He waited nervously for her to return. Something awful had happened to Ms. Jones and he needed to talk to Joules about it.

To calm himself, Kevin sat on his cot and wrote in his notebook. He was adding items to his Things to Avoid list, which had grown significantly since his arrival at Camp Whatsitooya. He suspected his list might grow much longer during the week, and this secretly worried Kevin. As usual, when something worried Kevin, he calmed himself by working on his list of Things to Avoid. It looked like this:

THINGS TO AVOID
The dark
School sloppy joes
Tom Bosco after eating the school's sloppy joes
Joules when she's mad

Joules when she's tired
Joules when she's cranky
Bananas
Slugs
Banana slugs
Stinky boulders
Spas
Avery
Canoeing
Canoeing with Avery

Kevin underlined the last item in case he was ever tempted to canoe with Avery again. Even though being towed behind a surfboard was pretty fun, canoeing had not been the adventure he had expected. But then, not much about Camp Whatsitooya had turned out as he had expected. Still, it was probably better than hanging out at the SPAMfest and being forced to taste test strawberry SPAMcake or SPAMchip oatmeal cookies or the dreaded kiwi SPAMshake.

Kevin flipped the page to start his new chart of Annoying Movie Characters. He thought of the people he had met during the last two days. Ms. Jones would make a very annoying movie character. She was like the hobby-hound in the movie *Crustacean!* who was too focused on his duck-carving to pay attention to the giant lobster that was about to attack. On the upside, characters like that usually had very interesting ways of leaving the movie. ("Leaving a movie" is a nice way of saying getting wiped out, which is also a nice way of saying pushing up daisies, kicking the bucket, assuming room temperature, or taking a dirt nap, which is also a nice way of saying . . . well . . . you know.)

In Ms. Jones's case, it would probably involve glitter.

Kevin felt a pang of guilt. It wasn't very nice thinking of people he actually knew as if they were movie characters. Especially after they have just been dragged away by a ferocious-looking white beast. And yet . . .

Nelson poked his head into the tent. He was carrying a tray with two plates of food.

"I brought you some tube steaks," he said. "You guys should avoid the café tonight. Everybody is mad at you for eating all the marshmallows."

"We didn't eat all the marshmallows," said Kevin, grabbing a plate from the tray and tearing into a hot dog.

"That's what I told them," said Nelson. "But nobody

believes me. It's okay, though, because I heard that Ms. Jones ordered a whole truckload of marshmallows for tomorrow. And candy for breakfast."

"You saw Ms. Jones?" asked Kevin.

"Yeah," said Nelson. "She came into the tent as I was leaving. She told Jammer that there was not enough sugar in our diets."

"Really?" said Kevin. "That's weird."

"I love sugar," continued Nelson, "but Mom says it makes me jumpy. Sometimes it makes me repeat myself over and over again and again and again. Does sugar make you jumpy or repeat yourself over and over and ov—"

Kevin tried to give Nelson the stink-eye, but he wasn't very good at it. He jotted a reminder to ask Joules for lessons.

"Is your eyeball okay?" asked Nelson. "It's kind of weird and twitchy. Sometimes my eye gets twitchy if I eat too much sugar. Then I get all jumpy and repeat myself and—"

Joules burst into the tent and flopped huffing and puffing onto her cot.

"Where were you?" asked Kevin. "Something horrible happened to Ms. Jones. She was dragged away by some great big hairy thing! But now she's back and she's acting weird."

Joules took a big breath and grabbed the second plate from Nelson.

"I saw her," said Joules.

She told them about her trip to the woods and Commander Jones.

"That's too bizarre," said Kevin. "And that's not all. Tell Joules what you heard, Nelson."

Nelson told her about the candy and marshmallow shipments.

"And we're not making any more lanyards at Craftland!" he added.

"No more lanyards?" asked Joules. "What will the campers make with all those supplies?"

"A three-stage intergalactic rocket with satellite communications," said Nelson very seriously. "We're going to need a whole lot of Popsicle sticks."

Chapter 26

The next morning, the twins met Nelson at Café du Lac. There was no bacon smoke wafting through the air, and there were no counselors frying bacon or flipping pancakes on the giant griddle. Instead, the griddle had been replaced by three giant vats of sugary cereal in colors not normally found in nature. Boxes of candy bars and crates of marshmallows were stacked up to the ceiling of the tent.

Joules and Kevin each filled two bowls with cereal and grabbed cartons of milk, then sat together at a picnic table by the door. This was a real treat for the twins who rarely had the chance to eat cereal at all, let alone cereal that was 100 percent guaranteed to rot your teeth. Nelson filled a bowl and sat down, too.

The rest of the campers sat at the other tables. They whispered and glared at the twins.

Commander Jones entered. Even though the light was dim inside the tent, she wore her sunglasses. She grabbed a box of candy bars and walked to the table where SmellyCat and Sparkletooth were giggling. Commander Jones smiled a weird stiff kind of smile in which her lips moved but her teeth remained clenched.

"Very sweet," she said in her robotic tone. "Excellent. Excellent. Keep eating."

Kevin rubbed his eyes, then squinted at the commander.

"She's so weird and blurry," he said.

"She really is—," Joules began, but she stopped when Commander Jones walked to their table. Though "walked" is not quite accurate. She reached their table in a swift half-gliding, half-hopping motion. Commander Jones looked blankly from Joules to Kevin to Nelson.

"You are the Rockman boy and girl, and that other child," she said, pointing slowly at Nelson.

"Your energy readings are very low," she said. "You must eat more. It is important to have energy so you can participate in the many fun and enjoyable camp activities available here at Camp Whatsitooya on the shores of scenic Lake Whatsosmelly. Camp Whatsitooya, providing youths exceptionally exceptional outdoor experiences. No exceptions."

She gave her stiff smile, which made Kevin's face hurt just looking at her. Then she tilted her head to one side and dumped the entire box of candy onto the table.

"Eat," she said.

"Uh—" said Joules. "Actually, we're late for a hike. Gotta go! Thanks for the snacks!"

Joules, Kevin, and Nelson grabbed some candy bars and dashed out of the tent. (Hey! Free candy is free candy. Even when it comes from a creepy, cyclone-haired craft queen with hot glue guns set to "stun"!)

"That was too freaky," said Kevin.

"Well, it must be freaky day at Camp Whatsitooya," said Joules.

"What?" asked Kevin, but one look toward the lake told him the answer.

Walking toward them was Counselor Blech, ready for a hike.

Chapter 27

Joules, Kevin, Nelson, and the other campers gathered outside Café du Lac for their nature hike with Counselor Blech.

"Nature is your enemy!" said Counselor Blech. "Remember this and you might survive. Forget this, and you'll be wiped out faster than bacteria in a bleach factory."

SmellyCat giggled, but Joules noticed it was a nervous giggle without the usual snort.

Counselor Blech was not what you could call a nature lover. He was a theoretical physicist. He loved theories. He did *not* love theories put into practice. That was the whole problem with nature. It was so real. So practical. Sure, it sounded good, but then there were the bloodsucking insects with their beady, buggy eyes and the poisonous plants climbing up every rock and boulder and the suspicious sounds of creatures hiding behind leaves and branches, waiting, *always* waiting with their sharp fangs and keen senses of smell, ready to attack when you least expect it and then so quick to devour their unsuspecting . . .

. . . Oh, sorry . . .

Got carried away there. Suffice it to say, Counselor Blech was a camp counselor not because he loved nature, but because he needed a job. He had previously been employed at a top-secret nuclear research facility somewhere in the Midwest. (451 Uranium Parkway, Batavia, Illinois. It's disguised as a Chuck E. Cheese's.)

The reasons Counselor Blech left his job were vague, but they involved some kind of super-conducting, super-colliding, super-dee-duper-holy-cow-that-was-one-wicked-big-explosion kind of event that left him reading the want ads for Camp Whatsitooya.

"My request for biohazard jumpsuits has been denied . . . again," he said with an exasperated sigh. "If anyone has failed to complete a next-of-kin notification, please do so now. We will wait."

No one left the group, but Jack, Eric, and Avery looked like they wanted to jump out of their sneakers and hide under their bunks. SmellyCat and Sparkletooth scooted closer together and squeezed one another's hands. They giggled in a higher pitch than usual and bobbed up and down at a frantic pace.

"Any questions?" asked Counselor Blech.

"Aren't we just hiking around camp?" asked Kevin. "I

mean, you make it sound kind of intense. How long will we be gone?"

"We should be back in twenty minutes," said Counselor Blech. "That is, *if* we make it back."

He turned on his heels, nearly smacking Nelson in the head with his giant flyswatter, and strode down the path toward the woods. For a highly overdressed scientist, he moved fast. The kids had to hustle to keep up with him as he blazed a path through the tall ferns and into the dim woods.

"Can we slow down a little?" asked Joules.

"That would increase our exposure to the dangerous forest fumes," Counselor Blech said nervously.

Joules took a deep breath of the calm forest air with its rich, earthy aroma and faint scent of honeysuckle.

"It smells good to me," she said.

Counselor Blech stopped hard, sending the chain of campers colliding into one another like so many electrons in a physics experiment gone bad.

"It smells good?" he asked in disbelief. "Do you know what's in this air? Spores. Millions of microscopic fungal spores waiting to find a hospitable host to settle on so they can sprout into new mushrooms and decompose everything in their reach. EVERYTHING!!!! And then there's the pollen. It's everywhere. The plants spew it into the air and wait for unsuspecting hikers to breathe it in so it can irritate their mucus passages and sinuses, causing a facial seizure that will release millions of bacteria into the atmosphere to be breathed in by other hikers. Does that smell good to you, Miss Rockman?"

"Uh—" said Joules. "So you are worried that we'll grow mushrooms or maybe sneeze because of some pollen?"

"Sure, you make it sound safe," said Counselor Blech. "But that's just what the spores want you to think!"

He gave Joules a scowl, then turned away and marched even faster into the woods.

The counselor moved so fast that the younger kids had to run to keep up. Finally, Jack, who was the smallest of the hikers, stopped and leaned against an enormous chestnut tree.

"Wait!" he yelled.

The hikers slammed on the brakes, and Counselor Blech pushed back through the group.

"What are you doing?" he asked Jack in a terrified voice. "Don't touch that overgrown *Castanea dentata*!" (That's a chestnut tree, for those of you who have forgotten your Latin.) "You could push it over and crush us all, and besides, you don't know where that tree has been!"

Kevin looked at the enormous tree and the puny kid leaning against it.

"It's a tree," he said. "Hasn't it been in the same place a really, really long time?"

The thought made Counselor Blech visibly upset.

"Think of it!" he shrieked. "It might have been there for decades. Centuries even! Imagine the millions of organisms that have touched it. Crawled upon it. Chewed on it! And worse!"

He narrowed his eyes suspiciously. His voice grew quieter. The whole forest seemed to hold its breath. Tears welled up in Jack's eyes and Avery looked ready to faint.

"Even now, thousands of organisms could be hiding in its branches waiting. Waiting and watching. Watching and waiting for unsuspecting prey to pass by and then . . ."

CRASH!!!!!

A giant white creature bolted out from behind the tree and ripped through the underbrush.

"HELLLLP!!!!" cried Counselor Blech, tearing off his mosquito netting, tossing his flyswatter into the air, and running like a maniac into the woods.

"HELLLLP!!!!" cried Avery, Eric, and Jack, running one way.

"HELLLLP!!!!" cried Sparkletooth and SmellyCat, running the other way.

"Let's go!" said Joules, picking up a stick and running after the beast with Kevin and Nelson right behind her.

The creature tore through the brush, leaving a trail of battered ferns and shrubs in its wake. At one point, Joules caught a glimpse of the beast's white fluffy fur and its blackened rump as it zigged and zagged through the underbrush, then it was gone.

The kids stopped. There was something in the path. Something large and metal.

Now imagine pulling this object out of the ground, cleaning it off, sticking it on a distant planet in another galaxy. Add some Fierce, Large, Ugly, and Ferocious Furballs, and voila!

Ring a bell?

Chapter 28

"Wow!" said Nelson.

"You can say that again," said Kevin.

"Wow!" said Nelson. "It's an F-Class Intergalactic Recon Probe."

"A what?" asked Joules, looking at Nelson in disbelief.

"You know. An F-Class Intergalactic Recon Probe. They were used to explore different solar systems back in the 1970s," said Nelson. "Wow. Wait until I tell Mom!"

He beamed.

"How do you know that?" asked Joules.

"I saw it on the Amazing Engineering Feats of the Universe Channel," said Nelson. "Next to the Plumbing Channel, it's my favorite! Mom says all the cool kids watch those kinds of shows. Maybe you should, too."

He gave Joules a you-could-use-a-little-improvement-in-the-cool-department kind of look.

Joules gave him the stink-eye.

Nelson smiled weakly.

"Check it out!" said Kevin, yanking open a metal

hatch and sticking his head inside the burned-out rocket.

Joules and Nelson looked inside.

"This hasn't been here long," said Kevin. "There's no rust."

"Sweet!" said Joules.

A gloved hand reached past Kevin and into the opening and wiped a little soot from the wall of the rocket.

"AAAAAAAH!" yelled Kevin and Joules, jumping away from the rocket.

The gloved hand belonged to Counselor Blech. His goggles were darkened and he swayed slowly back and forth.

Counselor Blech rubbed the soot on his tongue.

"It is not sweet," he said in a monotone voice. "It is not useful."

He tilted his head to one side and looked from Joules to Kevin to Nelson.

"You must improve your energy levels. Return to camp and refuel," he said.

"We were just going to do that," said Joules, tugging at Kevin's and Nelson's elbows.

"Let's get out of here," she whispered to the boys.

The three kids backed up a few steps, then turned and ran for camp.

They ran until they reached the shore of the lake, then stopped to catch their breath. Nelson was on the edge of panic. He looked anxiously from Kevin to Joules. They were out of breath but calm.

"Something has happened to Ms. Jones and Counselor Blech," said Nelson. "Something bad. It's like they are under some kind of spell."

"You're right," said Kevin. "We've seen things like this before. Reminds me of what happened in *It Came from the Mall*."

"Oh, yeah," said Joules. "And *Death Gator*. Remember that one?"

"Absolutely," said Kevin. "And *Attack of the Sponge People*."

"That one was classic," said Joules.

In fact, Kevin and Joules had seen many cases like this in the movies. Cases in which normal (or mostly normal) people changed drastically in a short time. A number of things could be the cause of the transformation, but one thing was for sure: It always meant trouble. Big, big trouble.

"We've got to tell someone!" said Nelson.

"Not really," said Joules. "It never works to tell someone."

"What do you mean?" asked Nelson. "We *have to*! Look! There's Jammer. He'll help. He'll know what to do!"

Jammer stood waxing his surfboard on the shore close to camp. Kevin and Joules watched as Nelson ran to the surfer and tapped him on the shoulder. Jammer turned slowly. He was wearing dark glasses and tilted his head to the side as he slowly swayed back and forth. Even from such a long distance, Kevin and Joules could hear Nelson yell.

"Help!!!!!"

"Famous Last Words," said Joules.

"Yep," said Kevin. "Famous Last Words."

Chapter 29

Nelson was already in their tent when Kevin and Joules arrived. More specifically, he was hiding under Joules's cot.

"Come out, Nelson," said Kevin. "It's okay."

"No, it's not!" squeaked Nelson.

"That's true," said Joules. "But I want to sit down, and you'll get squished."

"Oh," said Nelson, shimmying out from under the cot. "Sorry."

"Hey," said Joules. "I have an idea. Grab those containers under my cot and take them to the trash."

"Will that help?" asked Nelson.

"Oh, yeah," said Joules. "Absolutely."

"I'll do it!" said Nelson bravely, grabbing the containers and bolting out of the tent.

"How is taking out your trash going to help?" asked Kevin.

"It won't," said Joules, "but I didn't want to touch it. Did you?"

"Good point," said Kevin.

Kevin had been keeping a careful eye on the containers from his own cot, and they were definitely getting ripe and probably very dangerous. Mom's lunches were bad when they were fresh. Who knew what power that sauce had after festering in a hot tent. Still, he felt a little bad for Nelson. (But not bad enough to take the trash out himself.)

Nelson came back.

"I did it!" he said. "But one of the containers exploded and got some goop on my shoe."

"Ewww," said Kevin.

"Try not to lick that spot," said Joules, looking at the sizzling glob of goo on Nelson's sneaker.

"We need to tell someone about the counselors!" said Nelson. "We should hike to town and get help! It's only fifteen miles."

"Naw," said Joules. "That never works. That's what they thought in *Attack of the Clown People*. The two kids stole unicycles and tried to warn the townsfolk about the evil clowns that were about to kill them. Of course, everybody thought the kids were just clowning around and sent them back."

"What happened?" asked Nelson.

"They got stuffed into a clown car with sixty-three other bozos," said Kevin. "They came out wearing big shoes and red noses."

"Oh," said Nelson.

"It almost worked in that movie *Lagoon Man*," said Kevin in an attempt to reassure Nelson. "Everybody believed the kids, and they tried to escape in a big bus."

"Then what happened?" asked Nelson hopefully.

"The bus crashed into the swamp, and they all grew gills and became Lagoon People."

"Oh," said Nelson weakly. "What will we do?"

"The obvious thing," said Joules. "Let's eat."

Chapter 30

Kevin had opened his notebook and was furiously jotting notes as they sat in the Café du Lac.

"Do we have to be here?" whispered Nelson from across the table. "What if the counselors come in?"

"Look," said Kevin, "there are things we know and things we need to find out."

Kevin had drawn a line down the center of the paper, creating two columns. In the left column, he had started a list of "What We Know." The other side he had labeled "What We Don't Know but Better Find Out Before It's Too Late." It was a tight squeeze, but he managed to make the title fit.

The chart looked like this:

WHAT WE KNOW	WHAT WE DON'T KNOW BUT BETTER FIND OUT BEFORE IT'S TOO LATE
• We are not dead . . . yet. • The counselors have gone wacky.	• Who or what is controlling the counselors? • Where do they come from? • What do they want? • What's with all the marshmallows and candy? • Can we stop them and still keep the candy?

"Way to take charge," said Joules. "You guys work

with your paper and stuff, and I'm going to go take my handy-dandy stick and get some answers."

Joules walked to the table where SmellyCat and Sparkletooth were giggling, snorting, and chatting away about crafts as usual. Jack, Eric, and Avery were at the next table laughing and talking about surfing.

Jammer, Counselor Blech, and Commander Jones entered. They wore sunglasses, looked tired, and walked slowly toward the vats of cereal and stacks of candy and marshmallows. Kevin noticed that the store of "food" was only half as big as it had been that morning. He made a note under "What We Know."

Nelson was sitting with his feet sticking into the aisle. As Jammer passed, his foot brushed against Nelson's sneaker. Jammer jerked back his foot as if stung.

"Grrrrrrrrr, dud. That hurt," said Jammer.

"Don't you mean 'dude'?" asked Nelson.

"That's what I said, dud," said Jammer.

Commander Jones opened a crate of Marshmallow Fluff. She handed a jar to Jammer and one to Counselor Blech and took one for herself. In unison, they unscrewed the lids, raised the jars to their mouths, and gulped down the thick, white goop. They drained the jars, wiped their mouths with the backs of their hands, leaned back, opened their mouths, and . . .

. . . BUUUUUURRRRRP.

The burp blew through the lantern hanging from the ceiling.
WHOOOOOSH!

A ball of flame shot through the roof of the tent.

Kevin and Nelson stared in amazement, but nobody else seemed to notice. The giggling and chattering campers did not even blink at the booming sound or ball of fire that left a hole in the tent.

The counselors wiped their mouths again with the backs of their hands, grabbed new jars of Marshmallow Fluff, and started chugging. Within moments, the entire crate of Marshmallow Fluff was gone.

Joules came back to the table and scooted into the seat next to Nelson.

"What did you find out?" asked Kevin.

"Nothing," said Joules. "Absolutely nothing."

"Oh, c'mon!" said Kevin. "You found out something."

"Nothing!" said Joules. "And I mean *nothing*. Nobody even remembers the hike. They all say they were surfing with Jammer and making crafts with Commander Jones. It's like they never left camp."

Chapter 31

That afternoon, all the campers were summoned to Craftland. Even though Joules was on "craft probation," she went to gather clues with Kevin and Nelson.

The campers of Camp Whatsitooya squeezed onto the benches of the picnic tables, which were loaded with boxes of feathers, Popsicle sticks, and bottles of glitter glue.

Sparkletooth sat beaming at the end of the table next to SmellyCat. Sparkletooth had a whole new supply of glitter clinging to her teeth and clothes, and she sparkled in the afternoon sun. She could hardly contain her excitement at doing a new craft project, and bounced up and down and jiggled her feet wildly under the table.

Commander Jones and Jammer arrived.

"We have decided that Earth—we mean Camp Whatsitooya—is a logical place to conduct our primary mission. By mission, we mean fun athletic activities such as world domination," said Commander Jones.

Jammer elbowed her in the ribs and mumbled something to her.

"Oh," said Commander Jones. "We do not mean world domination. World domination is bad."

She smiled stiffly.

"Very bad," Jammer added, smiling stiffly, too.

"Also, we no longer require a three-stage intergalactic rocket. We now require a 103-inch plasma television with Dolby surround sound and a built-in gaming system," said Commander Jones.

"And a La-Z-Boy recliner," said Jammer. "With cup holders."

This time, Commander Jones elbowed Jammer in the ribs.

"What?" he asked. "Cup holders are very useful."

"Two La-Z-Boy recliners with cup holders," said Commander Jones.

"We have pipe cleaners," said Jammer, dumping a huge box of colored pipe cleaners onto the picnic tables.

Joules, Kevin, and Nelson watched in amazement. The other campers giggled as they grabbed at the pipe cleaners and started twisting them together and gluing feathers to the ends. They seemed to find the request to build a television from pipe cleaners completely normal.

Counselor Blech arrived. His shirt and hair were

covered with small globs of Marshmallow Fluff and candy.

"We have a problem with the food," he said nervously.

"What food?" asked Commander Jones.

"That's the problem," said Counselor Blech. "Someone ate it. I think it was the Earth frogs."

"What Earth frogs?" asked Commander Jones suspiciously. "I didn't see any Earth frogs."

"Er—the *invisible* Earth frogs?" said Counselor Blech. "They are very ferocious. And hungry."

"Use the Earth telephone device to find more food," said Jammer.

Counselor Blech squirmed.

"They ate that, too," he said. "They are very bad frogs."

At that moment, Sparkletooth waved and smiled sweetly at Commander Jones.

"That reminds me," said Jammer. "I am hungry."

"I have an idea," said Commander Jones.

"Burp," said Counselor Blech.

The three counselors whispered back and forth for a few moments. Then, at precisely the same instant, they tilted their heads to one side, looked at Sparkletooth, and smiled.

Chapter 32

Sparkletooth was not at dinner.

"Where's Sparkletooth?" Joules asked SmellyCat.

"Toothsparkwho?" asked SmellyCat.

"Mitzy?" asked Joules.

SmellyCat shrugged.

"Commander Jones," Joules said, "where's Mitzy?"

"The pink girl has returned to her school," said Commander Jones.

"Was something wrong?" asked Joules. "How did she feel?"

"Delicious," said Counselor Blech.

"Crunchy," said Jammer.

Commander Jones whacked the two counselors on the back of the head.

"Not crunchy and delicious," they said at the same time. "We mean fine."

"The pink girl felt ready for school after a summer of exceptional experiences here at Camp Whatsitooya."

Kevin, Joules, and Nelson shot worried looks to one

another. They didn't know which was weirder, Sparkletooth being gone or the counselors thinking they would fall for such a lame excuse.

Kevin noticed that the vats of cereal were nearly empty and the crates of marshmallows and candy were low. Also, the counselors were very energetic and did not speak to one another, but they seemed to communicate simply through looks and head motions and occasional head whacks. Also, they seemed bigger than before and far less blurry. Kevin wrote this in his chart. He noticed something else, too. Each time SmellyCat's giggles and snorts rose above the din of the other campers in the dining tent, Commander Jones, Counselor Blech, and Jammer all tilted their heads ever so slightly to the left. And they smiled.

Chapter 33

It was after midnight. A full moon shined down upon Lake Whatsosmelly, bathing its glassy surface in silver light. It was a scene from a postcard. Or, as Kevin Rockman thought, a scene from a movie. *The Werewolf of Lake Doom,* to be exact.

It had taken Kevin a long time to fall asleep. He was worried. Neither of the twins believed the story about Sparkletooth going back to school.

Still, they didn't know what to do. They had contemplated exploring the woods during the night to look for clues, but had decided it was too risky. Besides, they would have more success hunting in the daylight. Kevin was extremely glad to be on his cot instead of in the woods being watched by killer owls, rabid skunks, and the freaky white beast that dragged off Ms. Jones and probably Jammer and Counselor Blech.

When at last sleep arrived, it was a fitful sleep. Kevin's dreams were crowded with images of the day. Giant chestnut trees. Burned-out rockets. Swaying counselors and terrified campers. But one image in particular came back over and over. It was an image that disturbed Kevin more than all the others: the frozen smiles on the counselors' faces when SmellyCat laughed.

Thunk.

A strange noise woke Kevin. He sat bolt upright on his cot, his heart racing.

Thunk.

He heard it again. It came from somewhere among the tents.

"Joules—" he started.

"I heard it," said Joules, who was already out of her cot, pulling on her shoes and reaching for her stick. "Let's get Nelson."

Joules slipped out of the tent. Kevin flipped on the flashlight and followed her. It was bright enough in the moonlight to see without the flashlight, but Kevin was glad to have it. The twins stopped at Nelson's tent.

"Nelson!" whispered Joules. "Wake up."

"What, Mom?" asked Nelson.

"Oh, brother," Joules said, poking him with the stick. "Put on your shoes. We need you."

"Huh?" said Nelson, sitting up and looking around for his shoes.

Thud.

CLUNK.

"It's over by SmellyCat!" cried Kevin.

Kevin and Joules ran for SmellyCat's tent, followed by Nelson, who was half running, half hopping, trying to pull on his sneakers as he went. SmellyCat slept in the large tent at the center of camp.

Joules reached the tent first. She shook the canvas wall.

"Hey!" she said. "Are you guys okay? Wake up!"

No answer.

"Hey!" she repeated.

She pulled back the tent flap. Kevin shined his flashlight inside. The girls were gone.

"We've got to get the others," said Kevin, running to Jack and Avery's tent. Nelson ran to check on Eric.

Kevin pulled back the tent flap. Jack and Avery were gone.

"It's empty!" he called to Joules.

Joules yelled, "Nelson, what about Eric?"

Silence.

"Nelson?" yelled Joules.

Silence.

"NELSON!" yelled Kevin.

Joules and Kevin ran to the tent where Nelson should have been. It was empty and Nelson was gone. Kevin's flashlight beam landed on a shoe. More precisely, it landed on a smelly red sneaker with an odd-shaped spot that seemed—somehow—to glow in the dark.

Chapter 34

"NELS—!" yelled Kevin.

"SHHHHH!" whispered Joules. "What are you doing?"

"We've got to find Nelson," said Kevin.

"I know," said Joules. "But be quiet! Do you want them to find—"

As she spoke, a large figure behind her blocked the moon and cast a shadow that swallowed her and Kevin. It was unlike any shadow she had ever seen. Joules hoped it was just a trick of the breeze and the trees, but knew better. The shadow was broad. It was tall. And it was bunny-shaped.

"Too late," said Kevin in a squeaky thin voice.

"Ha!" yelled Joules, twirling around and jabbing her stick at the figure behind her.

"Ha," laughed Commander Jones, grabbing Joules's stick and snapping it in two.

"Ha. Ha. Ha," said Counselor Blech. "Why are we laughing?"

"Shut up," said Commander Jones.

"Ha. Ha. Ha. That's a good one," said Counselor Blech. "Ha. Ha. Ha. Ha. . . ."

Counselor Blech laughed so hard he fell against Commander Jones, knocking them both over.

"You idiot!" yelled Commander Jones.

"Run!" yelled Joules.

Joules and Kevin ran between the tents, jumping over the guy-wires and dodging the low branches that dipped onto the path. They were almost to Café du Lac when Joules looked back over her shoulder to see—

BAM!

She ran full force into the enormous figure that hopped out of the shadows. Joules fell backward, knocking Kevin to the ground and landing in a heap beside him.

"Duds," said Jammer in a robotic voice. "That was not cool."

Jammer reached down and scooped Joules up under his left arm and Kevin under his right. Where his arms touched the kids, a strange thing happened. Like a faulty hologram, his skin flickered and faded, revealing white fur. His hands morphed into large ferocious paws with sharp claws.

In a few enormous hops, he carried the twins to

Craftland, where Commander Jones and Counselor Blech were waiting. Jammer plopped Joules and Kevin onto the picnic table. As he released them, his fur and paws morphed back into skin-covered hands.

"They have seen my disguise," said Jammer. "It malfunctioned."

"No matter," said Commander Jones. "We no longer require these illusions."

The three counselors took off their sunglasses, revealing large, swirly eyes that glowed softly and turned in opposite directions. For a moment, the counselors' bodies flashed brighter, then dimmer, then brighter again. Finally, their human bodies faded away like the last flickers of a movie in a dark theater. Left in their place were the forms of three Fierce, Large, Ugly, and Ferocious Furballs . . . with fangs. Fluffs.

Chapter 35

At this point, you might be wondering how the Fluffs managed to assume the counselors' identities so completely and how their ability to project this illusion works. While it would be possible (and very easy) to explain this in scientific terms, it would also be dull. Instead, everyone go get a snack and a nice pillow and let's settle in for a lovely story time. Ready? Okay. Here we go. . . .

Once upon a time, there was a planet of Fierce, Large, Ugly, and Ferocious Furballs who spent their days hopping around, eating small creatures, and burping. The Fluffs were wondrous creatures with the ability to eat another creature and then assume that creature's appearance. (This involves the scientific process of absorbing the creature's DNA and using it to project a holographic field around the Fluff via the hollow tubules of the Fluff's fur. This procedure requires large quantities of sugar to sustain the holographic illusion and is rarely used by Fluffs, who would rather spend their energy burping. That is the scientific explanation. However, that sounds boring in a story so we're going to say they use magic! That's more fun, isn't it?) Okay, so where were we?

Oh, yeah. So, one day a Fluff was hopping around the planet eating small creatures when he got a great idea.

"I'll eat a small creature and use magic to look like it. None of the other Fluffs will know who I am. It will be so funny," he thought.

The Fluff ate a small creature and used his magic to look like the small creature.

"Hi!" he thought to the other Fluffs.

"Look," thought the other Fluffs. "Lunch!"

CHOMP.

Burp.

The end.

Chapter 36

"Let's put these earthlings into a more cooperative mood," said Commander Cottonswab.

The Fluffs' eyes spun round and round. Faster and faster, focusing their hypnotic energy on the twins. A faint woozy feeling came over Kevin. It reminded him of the feeling he'd experienced just yesterday while canoeing. He snapped his eyes shut.

"Close your eyes!" he yelled. "They're trying to hypnotize us."

Joules closed her eyes.

"You are no fun," said Counselor Blech. "But it does not matter. We do not need your energy. Tomorrow, we will have all the energy in the world!"

"And Sweden!" said Commander Jones. "Take them to the others."

The others! Joules and Kevin shot a glance at each other. Perhaps the counselors and campers were still alive.

Commander Jones (also known as Commander Cottonswab, for those of you who were wondering) and Counselor Blech (also called Floopsy by his friends) hopped toward the woods. The Fluff formerly known as Jammer (and even more formerly known as Moopsy) shoved the twins under his furry arms and hopped after them. From this point on, it is best that we call the Fluffs by their true names so we can eliminate any doubt that we are actually dealing with Fluffs.

Commander Cottonswab, Floopsy, and Moopsy sped down the path that followed the shore. Then they turned along a deer trail and directly into the deep forest. It was the very same path Joules had followed in search of the white beast from Café du Lac.

Just as Joules had been watched then by the yellow eyes of a lone crow, the strange parade of aliens and Earth children was watched now by the night eyes of the forest. From the safety of the shadows, the eyes of deer and owls, raccoons, and wildcats were fixed upon the Fluffs and their captives. Both the hunters and the hunted watched from the darkness.

And so did another creature. A creature with red hair, freckles, and one red sneaker.

Chapter 37

It might be valuable at this point to mention that when Moopsy snatched up Joules and Kevin back at Craftland, he picked them up feet first. As he ran through the woods, he carried them with their feet sticking out in front of him and the rest of them sticking out the back. It was an unfortunate choice for Moopsy because it gave the twins the opportunity to kick him in the face, which they did repeatedly. The Fluff tried blocking the kicking feet with his enormous floppy ears, but then he couldn't see where he was hopping, which caused him to crash into a tree, which was very annoying. This was the good part of this situation for the Rockman twins. The bad part was the view.

This view (and the fear that they were about to meet their impending doom) inspired Kevin and Joules to thrash, kick, and squirm wildly. As they struggled, Moopsy squeezed tighter, but his pace slowed. Within moments, Commander Cottonswab and Floopsy had hopped around a bend in the trail and were out of sight.

The woods were at their darkest here, but occasionally a break in the canopy let a shaft of moonlight reach the forest floor before being devoured by the ferns. Moopsy had just passed through one of these beams of moonlight when a figure stepped into the light and caught Joules's eye.

It was Nelson, carrying some kind of rope.

Joules whacked Kevin on the arm to get his attention and put her hands to her eyes as if she were wearing glasses.

"Where???" asked Kevin, who clearly got the message.

Joules pointed into the darkness behind them.

"Kick!" said Kevin, counting off with his fingers.

1 . . . 2 . . . 3.

WHAP!

Kevin and Joules sent their feet flying with a fury against Moopsy's face.

WHAP! WHAP! WHAP!

They kicked Moopsy in the nose as hard as they could, and for a moment, the Fluff stopped. The twins struggled to break free, but Moopsy's grasp was too great. In one swift (and surprisingly graceful) twirling motion, Moopsy flipped Joules and Kevin around so their feet were no longer a threat. What was a new threat for the twins was the Fluff's breath, which smelled like marshmallows. But not the sugary, mild sweetness of a brand-new fluffy white marshmallow. The Fluff's breath smelled like burned marshmallows. Burned marshmallows that have been stuck to a skunk's fur and left to mildew in a swamp for five months. It was not pleasant. It was worse than not pleasant. It was the kind of smell that had the power to make unicorns weep. Which, in case you didn't know, is powerful!

Moopsy's pit stop was brief. The entire maneuver took only a moment, but it was long enough for Nelson to catch up with the Fluff.

It's not exactly clear what Joules and Kevin expected their skinny, eleven-year-old friend to do against an enormous beast with fangs, claws, a viselike grip, and really, *really* bad breath. But they didn't expect what happened.

As Moopsy stopped to twirl Joules and Kevin about, Nelson ran past the Fluff without being noticed, waved at the twins, and vanished into the darkness.

Chapter 38

Once more, Moopsy started swiftly through the forest with Joules and Kevin clenched tightly in his armpits.

Directly ahead of them was the tall chain-link fence. Joules had seen this fence before, during her encounter with the transformed Ms. Jones. There was a narrow gash cut into the fence, which would allow them to get through. Even so, they would have to stop and squeeze through one at a time, and it would be a very tight fit for the Fluff. Trying to push through the gash at their current pace would jam the twins full force against the jagged metal, ripping them to shreds.

While the twins figured this out, Moopsy did not seem to. He did not stop. He did not slow down. The Fluff hopped faster and faster, and the fence grew closer and closer.

Moopsy was only three hops away from the fence. He moved faster.

Two hops. There was no way to stop now.

One hop.

Joules and Kevin covered their heads with their arms and braced themselves for the inevitable crash.

"AAAAAAAAAAAAHHHHHHH!!!!" they screamed.

Then Moopsy hopped.

In a single bounce, he cleared the fence and landed easily on the other side. (He is a rabbit, after all.) Without missing a beat, he continued down the path. Joules and Kevin lowered their arms and breathed out a sigh of relief.

The underbrush was thinner on this side of the fence and the trees were bigger. Ahead, they could just make out some kind of building and a light.

What happened next is best viewed in slow motion. Unfortunately, slow-motion books have not yet been invented, so you'll have to do this part yourself. Don't worry, it's easy. Just look at the following pictures *VERY,* **VERY** slowly.

BONK

MS. JONES WAS RIGHT.
YOU CAN NEVER HAVE
TOO MANY LANYARDS.

Chapter 39

"Hurry!" said Nelson, yanking Joules and Kevin up from the path. "They're coming."

Joules, Kevin, and Nelson tumbled into the forest and ducked behind a mulberry bush just as Floopsy and Commander Cottonswab came down the path. They found Moopsy face-first in the dirt.

"Why are you eating dirt?" thought Commander Cottonswab.

"I am not eating dirt," thought Moopsy. "Should I?"

"Only if you're going to share," thought Floopsy.

Moopsy stood up and rubbed his ears with one paw and his rump with the other.

"They got away," he thought.

Commander Cottonswab whacked the other two Fluffs.

"Forget those children," he thought. "They had insignificant amounts of energy. They are irrelevant."

"They are an elephant?" thought Moopsy.

"Shut up," thought Commander Cottonswab, whacking Moopsy.

"Got it," thought Moopsy.

"We must use our voices now and also rest to preserve our telepathic powers. We will need our powers when the satellite comes into range at dawn," said Commander Cottonswab. "Then we will use them to control the world and have the greatest feast ever!"

"Yum," said Floopsy.

"That reminds me," said Moopsy. "I'm hungry. Can we eat one of the small humans tonight? The pink ones look delicious."

"Their brains are not ready. They will not provide enough energy," said Commander Cottonswab. "Remember the last one? The brain was not ready."

"It was better than the dud man," said Moopsy. "He tasted like suntan lotion."

"The other man tasted like hand sanitizer," said Floopsy. "Blech."

"Can we just have a nibble?" asked Moopsy.

"No," said Commander Cottonswab. "They will be ready in the morning. After we begin the satellite transmission, we will feast. Now, we must return to camp and save our energy until dawn."

Commander Cottonswab whapped Moopsy and

Floopsy upside their furry heads with his enormous floppy ears and hopped back toward camp, disappearing into the darkness.

Moopsy and Floopsy followed the leader, hitting and kicking each other as they went. Long after the Fluffs had disappeared into the dark, Joules, Kevin, and Nelson could hear the sounds of things that go **slap**, **WHAP**, **WHOP**, **POP**, **smack**, **thwack**, and **bump** in the night.

Chapter 40

The kids waited a moment to catch their breath and make sure the Fluffs were not coming back before stepping out onto the path.

"Thanks, Nelson," said Kevin. "That was some kind of rescue."

"Yeah," said Joules, rubbing her elbow. "That was actually pretty good."

"You're welcome," said Nelson happily. "I knew I had to do something when those creatures showed up in camp. Now what?"

"We have to find the others," said Kevin. "I bet they're in that building."

"But first we need a plan," said Joules.

Kevin looked with surprise at his sister. She usually mocked his need to think through a situation before attacking it. Perhaps she had learned something from him after all.

Joules searched the ground and found a thick stick. She picked it up and took a few swipes at the air to test its strength and balance.

"Now that's a good plan," she said, pointing the stick toward the dim light coming from the building. "Let's go!"

The trio hurried down the path toward a run-down octagonal brick building surrounded by tall grass that had not been mowed in a long time. It was nearly to the kids' knees, but they barely noticed. Their attention was focused entirely upon a gigantic ear. Well, more accurately, a picture of a gigantic ear painted on a gigantic satellite dish that towered above the whole facility. A sign in front of the dish said:

> ### E.A.R.S.
> Earth-Alien Radio Satellite
> Director Dr. Donald J. Dewdy
> August 1, 1972

A huge "No Trespassing by order of the U.S. Government" sign was nailed to the door of the brick building. Kevin and Joules peered through the side windows. They could see light under a door across the lobby.

"Get a brick," said Joules. "We'll break the window and get in."

"I have a better plan," said Kevin, reaching for the doorknob. "Let's try the door."

He turned the knob and the door swung open.

"Lucky," said Joules.

Kevin smiled and led them inside. They heard the sound of voices and . . . was it . . .

Singing?

Chapter 41

Perhaps you have found yourself in a similar situation as Joules and Kevin and Nelson—trying to rescue a band of campers from killer alien rabbits bent on eating everyone on the planet while avoiding becoming lunch yourself. If so, what did you do? Really. This would be a great time to speak up because our heroes would really appreciate knowing.

Just sayin'. . . .

Chapter 42

The sound of singing came from behind a wooden door just off the lobby. Joules, Kevin, and Nelson crouched outside the door.

"Count of three," said Joules, raising her stick.

One . . .

Two . . .

THREE!

Kevin threw open the door and Joules jumped into the room, ready to strike.

"Omigosh," said Kevin.

"Wow," said Nelson.

"What?" asked Joules, dropping her stick.

The door opened onto a large, well-lit room with rows of television monitors and complicated control panels all facing an enormous screen at the front of the room. The kids had seen images of such a room on history shows about the space program. This was Mission Control.

Campers sat at the control stations, their unblinking

eyes spinning slowly in opposite directions as they stared at the monitors in front of them.

The same image was displayed on every monitor and on the enormous screen at the front of the room. For only a moment, the twins looked at the giant screen, but what they saw was so horrible, they had to look away.

"Those monsters! How could they make them watch such a thing?" Joules asked as two dozen young teens in gym clothes broke into a Broadway musical dance number about school lunches.

"*Junior High School Musical Seven*," said Kevin. "The horror."

"It's kind of catchy," said Nelson, who stared blankly at the screen, swaying along as a squeaky-voiced seventh grader sang, "Your love is like a Tater Tot. Sometimes cold and sometimes hot."

Joules punched Nelson on the arm.

"Snap out of it!" she said. "Don't you see what they're doing? They are trying to turn everyone's brain into sweet mush so they can eat them! You shut it off, and we'll get everybody out of here!"

"C'mon everybody!" Joules yelled at the campers.

No response.

"Hey!" said Kevin, shaking Avery by the shoulders. "You're in danger! Wake up!"

Avery stared at the dancing teens on his monitor with a sappy smile on his face. Kevin blocked his view of the screen, but Avery looked through Kevin as if he weren't there.

"The override is engaged," said Nelson. "I can't stop the transmission."

"My plan will stop it," said Joules, raising her stick.

"No, it won't," said Nelson. "This system is wired to keep running. If one thing breaks, the others keep going. The emergency backup is probably at some remote location."

"Why?" asked Joules.

"This is Mission Control. What if they had a rocket launch going and then a tornado or something hit this facility?" said Nelson. "They'd lose control of the rockets."

"Doesn't matter anyway," said Kevin, looking at the campers who smiled sweetly at the screens. "We're too late. They're zombies."

"There's something else," said Nelson nervously. "That satellite dish outside can send signals around the world if it syncs up with an orbiting satellite."

"That's what the aliens are doing!" said Kevin. "They're going to use that satellite to hypnotize people and make them an easy meal!"

"They're going to broadcast this show to the entire world!" said Joules. "This goop will turn everyone's brains to syrup! I guess there's only one thing to do."

"What?" asked Nelson.

"Let's find some food," said Joules. "I'm starving."

Joules walked back into the lobby. Kevin glared after her.

"I'm staying here," he said. "We can't just leave these guys!"

But at that moment, the cast of *Junior High School Musical Seven* broke into a song that was either about winning the big basketball game or dissecting frogs.

"You gotta have the guts to get the glory!" they sang.

Kevin shuddered.

"Wait for me!" he yelled, running out of Mission Control. "Wait for me!"

Chapter 43

Joules, Kevin, and Nelson searched the building, wandering down hallways and poking their heads into each room they passed. Most of the rooms were offices or defunct computer labs. Many of them still had furniture and books stacked in corners. A few still had papers on the desks, but it was clear that no one had been in the facility for a long time.

"This gives me the creeps, like that movie *Don't Look in the Bathroom!*" said Joules. "Remember the one where the students at a boarding school disappear one by one and the last kid goes into the bathroom and finds a killer zi—"

"Not the same," interrupted Kevin, pointing to a memo taped to the wall.

> Due to budget cuts, this facility will be phased out during the next two weeks. Minimal utilities for Mission Control will remain. Thank you for working for the U.S. Government. Please turn out the lights when you leave. Have a nice day.

In the basement, the kids found a large kitchen lined with cabinets. The kitchen counters were stacked high with heavy-duty cooking pots and boxes filled with foil-sealed white packets. Each packet was printed with black letters. "PEAS." "CARROTS." "ASPARAGUS." "BEEF STEW." "ICE CREAM."

"Astronaut food!" squealed Nelson, picking up a packet of beef stew and ripping the end open. "I saw a show about this once. This stuff is amazing, and it never goes bad!"

"Blech," said Joules. "It starts out bad!"

Joules hoisted herself onto a countertop and dangled her feet over the edge.

"Still," she said. "It's all we've got."

She plucked a packet of "ICE CREAM" from a box, broke off a piece of the chalky, freeze-dried pink square, and touched it to her tongue.

"Hey," she said. "That's pretty good."

"Hello!" said Kevin. "Kind of need a plan here. Or have you forgotten the situation we're in? We've got a room full of zombies up there and three aliens back at camp who could come here any minute. That's bad!"

"The aliens are recharging their telereceptors. Remember? They won't come back until dawn," said

Joules, hopping off the counter. "You boys figure out a plan, and I'll look around for something useful like a secret weapon and a vending machine."

Kevin opened his notebook to the list he and Nelson had started earlier. So much had happened since then. Nelson and Kevin talked about Sparkletooth, the Fluffs' disguises, and their awful breath.

"It's kind of weird how the aliens didn't like you and Joules," said Nelson. "I think you're nice."

"They didn't like you, either," said Kevin. "Remember when Jammer stepped on your foot? He acted like you bit him."

"It's a good thing I had my shoe on," said Nelson. "He might have broken my toe. I wish I had my shoe now. I miss my shoe."

"Stop worrying about your shoe," said Kevin. "The aliens don't care about your sh— Wait a minute. Maybe they do. When Jammer hit your foot and jerked away like it was poison, maybe it was your shoe!"

"Or something on my shoe!" said Nelson.

"That's it!" said Kevin. "It was the sauce! Remember the sauce that dripped on your shoe? The aliens hate the secret sauce! It's probably why they don't like us and why

Jammer's disguise melted when he touched me and Joules. Eating Mom's secret sauce probably mutated our DNA or something."

Joules did not hear this discussion. She had just walked into the pantry at the back of the kitchen and flipped on the light.

"Joules!" yelled Kevin. "I know just what we need to fight the aliens!"

"So do I!" Joules yelled back.

She was looking at the stack of crates that reached from the floor to the pantry ceiling.

SPAM!!!!!

Chapter 44

Kevin and Nelson ran to the pantry, where Joules stood with a can of SPAM in each hand.

"It's perfect!" she said, throwing a can at Kevin's head.

"Hey!" yelled Kevin, ducking out of the way. "That could kill a guy."

"Exactly!" said Joules. "All we need now is some kind of cannon or catapult or something. Maybe we can make one!"

"That could kill a *guy*," said Kevin. "But we're not talking about guys. We're talking about aliens. Ferocious, furry, fanged aliens with bad breath. But don't worry. I've got a plan!"

"Is it a good plan or a stupid plan that has lots of charts and diagrams and not much fighting?" asked Joules.

"It has a stick," said Kevin.

"Count me in!" said Joules.

Chapter 45

"Okay," said Joules. "Let's get cooking. If secret sauce freaks out the aliens, maybe it can stop them, too."

Kevin, Joules, and Nelson opened can after can of SPAM, draining the clear(ish) juice into the large copper soup pot on the stove. They left the cubes of meat in the metal cans and packed them back into the cartons. Next, they set to work ripping open packets of freeze-dried astronaut food. They opened packets of asparagus, beef stew, peas, and spinach and tossed them into the pot. The mixture turned a disgusting greenish brown as the astronaut food dissolved and the secret sauce started to boil.

"This will be good," said Joules, pulling out a new case of freeze-dried food. "And by good, I mean good and deadly! Just like Mom makes!"

She tossed in freeze-dried prunes, squash, rice pudding, and liver. The brew changed from a greenish brown to a purplish greenish brown and rapidly started to thicken.

"How will we know when it's done?" asked Nelson.

Splurp![*]

The molten sauce heaved and splurped, releasing a toxic, faint-purple vapor that knocked the campers back a few steps.

"IT'S DONE!!!!"

[*] **Splurp** is a rare sound made only by vats of SPAM juice and astronaut food bubbling in a thick, oozy, purplish greenish brownish molten lava kind of way. **Splurp** is not a good sound.

Chapter 46

"Hey, look at this," said Kevin, who had been reading a framed article hanging on the wall. Nelson and Joules came over to see. The article included a picture of two men in suits standing in front of a rocket exactly like the one the kids had seen in the forest. In fact, it *was* the very same rocket. Only the picture was taken a long time ago and the rocket was not, therefore, crunched and burned out and covered with bits of Fluff fur.

It was shiny.

Professor Donald J. Dewdy welcomes Governor Winkleheiny to the E.A.R.S. launch facility. E.A.R.S., which stands for Earth-Alien Radio Satellite, will launch its first reconnaissance rocket to the far reaches of space later this year. The rocket is equipped with sophisticated communication technologies and will send back reports of possible life-forms on other planets. After collecting sufficient soil, water, and atmospheric and life-form samples, the rocket will use its homing device to return to Earth, at which time scientists will determine if further contact with alien life is possible.

Professor Dewdy believes that we will contact alien life-forms in the very near future. When asked about Professor Dewdy's predictions, Governor Winkleheiny responded, "His name sounds like 'doody.'"

Professor Dewdy replied, "The search for intelligent life in the universe continues."

Remember this when you're grown up. It explains a lot about grown-ups.

Chapter 47

"Okay," said Joules. "So now we have a toxic death potion. How do we use it? It's not sweet, so they aren't going to drink it."

"I don't know," said Kevin. "What if we spray it on them?"

"Do you have a squirt gun?" asked Joules.

"Don't need one," said Nelson. "We'll use the fire sprinkler system! All we have to do is feed the goop into the right water lines, and when the sprinkler goes off, it will rain secret sauce! That's easy."

"You can do that?" asked Joules.

"I told you," said Nelson with an enormous grin, "all the cool kids watch the Plumbing Channel!"

"So I hear," said Joules. "So where does the stick come in?"

"Well . . . ," said Kevin sheepishly. "I kind of lied about that."

"I knew it," said Joules, giving Kevin a fake stink-eye. "That's why I've come up with Plan B!"

Kevin smiled as Joules started hauling drained cans of SPAM upstairs to Mission Control. Most people would be offended by a sister who felt the need to come up with a backup plan, but not Kevin. He had seen enough movies to know that you always need a Plan B. Sometimes a good Plan B can keep you from being squished by truck-sized cockroaches or gnawed on by a two-ton hamster. It stands to reason that when faced with ferocious alien bunnies, a Plan B is definitely a good idea. In fact . . .

"I'll get busy on a Plan C. Just in case," said Kevin, giving the sauce one last stir and heading upstairs with a box of astronaut ice cream.

Chapter 48

It was almost dawn when Nelson finished the plumbing work for Plan A. However, he could not test the sprinklers without using up all the secret sauce. There was enough secret sauce to get one—and only one—good shot at the aliens. If the sprinklers didn't go off when he flipped the manual switch, it was Plan B time.

Joules had been busy fortifying a corner of Mission Control for Plan B. She stacked SPAM cans into pyramids behind a semicircle of desks. From here, the kids could neutralize the rabbits by hurling cans at their heads. Joules had hoped to find a cannon or catapult sitting around. No luck. However, she did fashion a kind of SPAM chucker from her stick and a pair of dirty gym socks she found in the janitor's closet. It wasn't much, but it might help.

Besides the socks, Joules also found a bucket, some matches, and a mop handle. Kevin could use these for Plan C. There were three matches, and they were the big old-fashioned kind that would ignite when struck against any rough surface. That was the good news. The bad news was that they were the big old-fashioned kind that would ignite when struck against any rough surface. This meant Kevin had to be very careful not to light them by accident. And worse, it meant that they were old. V*ery* old. This type of match had been replaced by safety matches years ago. If they had absorbed too much moisture over the years, they would crumble and not light. And with only three matches, Kevin was afraid to test one. He crossed his fingers, bundled the matches together so they wouldn't snap off when struck, and used Nelson's lanyard to lash them to the mop handle. (If you've ever tried to do anything with crossed fingers, you'll know how hard that must have been!) Kevin spent the rest of the time opening packets of astronaut ice cream and crumbling the chalky cubes into the bucket.

At one end of Mission Control was a special area with a microphone and four cameras aimed at a large E.A.R.S. emblem on the wall. If the aliens planned to send a transmission to the world, this was where it was going to happen.

"What about them?" asked Joules, pointing to the smiling camper zombies.

"There's nothing we can do," said Kevin. "They won't

move, and we can't carry them. But we have to stop the aliens or these guys are on the menu!"

Junior High School Musical Seven had ended. As had its sequel and its sequel and its sequel and . . .

The zombified campers stared at *Junior High School Musical Thirty-three.* The same teen actors who had been singing about Tater Tots were now singing about graduation day. At least Joules thought they were the same kids. She was pretty sure one of them had grown a beard since the last time she looked.

A thirty-year-old cheerleader sang to a guy in a graduation gown, "Your love is like a graduation hat. Weird and square and sort of flat."

Joules groaned.

"This better work," she said. "Or we'll all turn to zombies. What happens if Plan A fails, Plan B fails, *and* Plan C fails?"

"There's always Plan D," said Kevin.

"What's Plan D?" asked Nelson.

"RUN!!!!!" said Kevin.

Chapter 49

Fluffs are many things. Fluffy. Ferocious. Fanged. And a little stinky. Okay, a lot stinky. But there is one thing they are not. Stealthy.

It was easy for the twins and Nelson to hear the Fluffs arrive at dawn. They spent five minutes whomping and stomping and whapping and slapping at one another in the lobby while trying to get through the doorway at the same time. As the aliens approached, Joules ducked behind her fort and Nelson crouched behind a chair at the back of the room, where he could pull the fire sprinkler switch at the right moment.

Kevin could not hide. For Plan C to work, he had to be close to the Fluffs. Very close. He stashed the bucket of freeze-dried ice cream and the "matchstick" beneath a control station next to the E.A.R.S. emblem and sat down. He pretended to be hypnotized. Like the zombified campers, he sat stiffly and stared blankly at the screen, where the actors were doing a montage of every single adventure they had shared during the last thirty-two movies about life in middle school.

The Fluffs threw open the door and tumbled into Mission Control snarling and slapping at one another with their long ears. They looked cranky, tired, and mean.

About time, thought Kevin, who could feel his brain turning to mush as a boy and girl with braces sang a duet: "I love the way your braces shine. Full of pizza just like mine."

The Fluffs tumbled onto the stage area in front of the cameras. They were just feet away from Kevin. They smacked their lips at the zombie campers.

"Delicious," said Commander Cottonswab. "Their brains are ready. We shall dine soon! First, we must begin our transmission."

"Once it is complete," said Moopsy, "all the crunchy sweet earthlings will be ours!"

At that moment, the movie flickered on the screen and went black, a light turned red above the four cameras, and the three Fluffs were projected onto the screen and command monitors.

Showtime.

Chapter 50

The lights on the control stations began to flash. Then, one by one, they stayed on. The remote connections were complete. Around the world, people were watching.

"The satellite is in range!" said Commander Cottonswab. "Smile."

Floopsy and Moopsy showed their fangs and waved at the camera. Their eyes began to swirl faster.

"Earthlings of Earth," said Commander Cottonswab. "Yes. We mean you. We are not here to conquer your delicious planet. That would be bad. Tasty, but bad."

He smiled his creepy fake smile while Floopsy and Moopsy shook their heads in the background.

"Bad," they said.

"Would you like to hear a joke?" Commander Cottonswab said flatly. "It is a funny one. You will like it. Ha ha. Come close to your television set and look into our eyes.

"That is the way. Closer . . . closer . . . ," said Commander Cottonswab, his eyes glowing brighter and brighter and swirling faster and faster.

"Look into our eyes!" he said. The Fluffs' eyes swirled so fast they throbbed. "The connection is made. You are now under our power. Ha ha ha ha. The joke is on you!"

"You must do as we say," said Moopsy. "Parents, feed your children candy. They must eat only candy and marshmallows to prepare them for the Brain Readiness Transmissions you call *Junior High School Musical*."

Kevin knew they had to interrupt the transmission before parents around the world started sugaring up their kids to become the ultimate alien buffet.

The Fluffs smacked their lips. But then a terrifying sound rose around Kevin as all of the zombie campers began to smack their lips, too.

Now, thought Kevin. C'mon, Nelson . . . Pull the switch!

He could not yell to Nelson without sacrificing any hope of his backup plan working. And he feared, in his gut, that they would need every plan they had to defeat the aliens.

Joules was also watching. She peeked over the barricade at the Fluffs.

"Now, Nelson!!!!" she yelled. "NOW!!!!"

Chapter 51

"I'm trying!" yelled Nelson.

In fact, the moment the Fluffs had moved into position on the stage and stood beneath the fire sprinklers, Nelson had jumped into action. He flipped open the plastic case that covered the switch and pulled on the lever. It would not budge. He pulled and tugged and whacked at it, but the switch was stuck.

At the moment Joules yelled his name, Nelson was whacking the switch with his sneaker. Also, at that moment, two other things happened.

1. Moopsy turned away from the camera and, in three horribly hasty hops, grabbed Nelson and flung the barefoot boy over his shoulder. Nelson banged his shoe against the Fluff's head, but the Fluff did not even notice. Plan A: FAILURE.

2. Floopsy hopped directly toward Joules, who grabbed the SPAMChucker and took aim. BAM! A can of SPAM smacked the Fluff in the eye.

Floopsy recoiled from the blow for just an instant, then hopped again. SMACK! Another can hit its target: Floopsy's nose. This time, Floopsy did not slow down. As Joules loaded the next can into the sock weapon, Floopsy scooped her up by the feet, tossed her over his shoulder, and in two hops was back to the stage. Plan B: EPIC FAILURE.

When Plan A and Plan B failed, Kevin knew that there was only one hope of stopping the aliens from eating all the humans in the world, and it was him. What he did not know, at that moment, was that the swirling eyes of the campers were trained like lasers right at his head.

Chapter 52

"Watch out!" yelled Joules as the lip-smacking zombies stood and closed in on Kevin, their outstretched arms clawing the air in front of them.

Kevin pulled the "matchstick" and bucket from beneath the control station and kicked at Avery. The zombie boy fell back, knocking Jack, Eric, and SmellyCat into a heap on the floor. Kevin jumped onto the stage.

"Hey Bunny Foo Foo!" he yelled. "Come and get it!"

"Dud!" said Floopsy. "I will come and get you."

"Smell this!" yelled Kevin, pushing the bucket of sweet-smelling astronaut ice cream into the Fluff's face.

"Mmmmm?" said Floopsy. "Yum."

Floopsy dropped Joules and grabbed the bucket from Kevin. In one tilt of his enormous paw, he dumped the ice cream into his mouth.

Kevin pulled Joules up from the floor and handed her the stick.

"Will you do the honors, sis?" he asked.

"Wha—" Joules started, but a deep rumbling grumbling noise began in Floopsy's belly.

Joules smiled at Kevin.

"Now that's a plan I like!" she said as the sound grew louder and rose higher and higher in the Fluff's body.

Like a golf pro, Joules swung the mop handle low, striking the matches on the floor and ending her stroke with a tiny flame six inches from Floopsy's face as the Fluff leaned back, opened wide, and . . .

BUUUUUURRRRRRPPPPPPPPPP!
WHOOOOOOOOOOOSSSSHHHHHHH!!!!!!!!!!!!

A ball of flame shot toward the ceiling.

Click.

Splsssshhhhhhhhhh.

The fire sprinkler was activated. Purplish greenish brown rain showered down upon Mission Control, drenching three heroes, a band of zombie campers, and the hollow fur of three very surprised Fierce, Large, Ugly, and Ferocious Furballs.

Chapter 53

The splurpy sauce splashed into the Fluffs' eyes, which swirled slower and slower until they stopped swirling completely. The sauce clogged the Fluffs' telereceptors, blocking their communication and at the same time making the Fluffs shrink. The process looked a lot like this:

Cottonswab silently twitched his cute bunny nose. Moopsy silently wiggled his cute bunny ears. Floopsy silently waggled his cute (and blackened) bunny tail.

Click.

The sprinklers shut off.

Standing in a puddle of purplish greenish brown splurp were three very soggy, very stunned, and very silent little bunnies with eyes that did not swirl at all.

Chapter 54

As the Fluffs lost the power to communicate, they also lost their power over the zombified campers. One by one, the campers snapped out of their daze and looked around.

"Where are we? What's going on? Why is it raining inside? Where did the TVs come from?"

"CanBunFluffUs?" asked SmellyCat, grabbing up the cute little bunnies on the stage and kissing them on the tops of their adorably cute little bunny heads.

"I don't know," said Joules. "Maybe it's okay if you don't let them eat any sugar. Wow! I speak GiggleSnort!"

Joules looked at Nelson and Kevin and smiled.

"JobGuysGood," she said.

"You too," said Nelson.

"Let's get everyone out of here," said Kevin.

The campers and three ridiculously adorable bunnies left Mission Control and headed back to Camp Whatsitooya on the shores of Lake Whatsosmelly, where they spent the day napping, swimming, and relaxing.

Chapter 55

The rest of the week at Camp Whatsitooya was everything the Rockman twins had hoped for in a summer camp and more. The campers, it turned out, were gifted chefs. Well, they were gifted pancake-makers, and that was fine with Joules and Kevin.

SmellyCat spent their days at Craftland bedazzling collars and beading lovely felt hats for the adorable little bunnies. Each day, they held bunny fashion shows beneath the elm tree and dressed the lovely creatures in sparkly pink and purple bunny dresses and made them dance by lifting the bunnies under the armpits and bouncing them up and down.

They fed the bunnies carrots and tiny cubes of SPAM. The bunnies growled a little, but got used to it.

Joules, Kevin, Nelson, and the rest of the campers split their time between the lake and the forest. They swam, sailed, canoed, hiked through the woods, and told ghost stories around the campfire. Kevin intended to work on his chart of Annoying Movie Characters or his list of Things to Avoid, but somehow, the days drifted by without much time to do so. And to his surprise, he was glad.

Joules and Kevin could have stayed at Camp Whatsitooya forever. But as all good things must come to an end, so must summer camps and SPAM festivals.

On Saturday morning, Joules and Kevin packed their bags and said good-bye to the other campers. Kevin got Nelson's address and promised to write.

"I bet you will, too!" said Nelson happily. "Mom says I'm a good judge of character, and I can tell you really will write!"

"I won't," said Joules. "I'll be busy watching the Plumbing Channel like all the cool kids I know."

She gently jabbed Nelson in the arm with her stick and Nelson grinned.

Joules and Kevin hiked past Stinky Boulder, through the deep woods, and back to the road where their parents had left them standing in the weeds seven short days before.

Chapter 56

"**How was camp?**" asked Mrs. Rockman as the family drove away from Camp Whatsitooya.

"Okay," said Joules.

"Did anything exciting happen?" asked Mr. Rockman.

"You know," said Kevin, "the usual camp stuff. Hiking. Canoeing. Saving the world from enormous alien rabbits with fangs."

"Wonderful," said Mrs. Rockman. "I knew you would learn about wildlife. I was thinking about next year's festival. How do we top our SPAMaphone surprise? This year we won because we dropped the phone into the batter and it went off during judging. Why don't we bake a speaker into a quiche next year and make it talk! In fact, we could . . ."

Kevin smiled at Joules, who rolled her eyes and smiled back. Joules put in her earphones, tilted her seat back, and closed her eyes. Kevin leaned against the window and watched the van's shadow slide along the edge of the road as they drove. The road followed the winding path of a small creek, and the van rocked gently this way and that, making

Kevin's eyelids grow heavier and heavier until—at last—he fell into a deep sleep.

Had Kevin and Joules been awake when the van climbed the hill that looked down on their hometown, they might have seen a strange object streak across the sky and disappear in a sudden flash of light in the woods. They might also have heard Mrs. Rockman wonder about that flash of light and hear Mr. Rockman's answer that it was probably nothing, and even if it was something, it probably couldn't hurt you, and besides, it was probably dead, so there was really no need to worry.

No need to worry.

Ah, yes.

Famous Last Words.

THIS BOOK WAS ART DIRECTED AND designed by Chad W. Beckerman. The text is set in 12-point Adobe Garamond, a typeface originally drawn by the sixteenth-century French engraver and punch-cutter Claude Garamond. Garamond modeled his typefaces on those created by Venetian printers at the end of the fifteenth century. The modern version used in this book was designed by Robert Slimbach, who studied Garamond's historic typefaces at the Plantin Moretus Museum in Antwerp, Belgium. The display font is House of Terror. The art was created by Dan Santat.